FICTION

CAUTION: MEN AT WORK
April Kelly 5

THE OBSOLETE
Richard Hallows 15

EXODUS
Jillian Grant Shoichet 22

REVERSION
Marcelle Dubé 30

TAM HINKLE'S LAST SUNDOWN
Richard Prosch 43

SOLD AT AUCTION
Nicolas Calcagno 50

THE CASE OF THE BEGUILED COURIER
J. R. Lindermuth 67

I SMELL A MYSTERY
Adrienne Stevenson 73

A BAD HARE DAY
A You-Solve-It by John M. Floyd 81

INQUIRIES & ADVERTISING

Address: Suite 22, 509 Commissioners Road West, London, Ontario, N6J 1Y5
Advertising: Email info@mysterymagazine.ca
Editor: Kerry Carter **Publisher:** Chuck Carter **Cover Artist:** Robin Grenville Evans
Submissions: https://mysterymagazine.ca/submit.asp
Mystery Magazine is published monthly by AM Marketing Strategies. The stories in this magazine are all fictitious, and any resemblance between the characters in them and actual persons is completely coincidental. Reproduction or use, in any manner of editorial or pictorial content without express written permission is prohibited. Copyright on stories remain with the artist or author. No portion of this magazine or its cover may be reproduced without the artist's or author's permission.

MYSTERY MAGAZINE

MYSTERY MAGAZINE.

SUBSCRIBE TO THE WORLD'S MOST-READ MONTHLY MYSTERY MAGAZINE FOR A FEW DOLLARS PER MONTH!

THE FUTURE OF SHORT MYSTERY FICTION

Subscribe to digital issues at MysteryMagazine.ca or buy paperback issues on Amazon.

Read mysteries on your phone by visiting mysterymagazine.ca/app

ANNUAL DIGITAL SUBSCRIPTION $29.95 USD

LIMITED TIME OFFER

CAUTION: MEN AT WORK

April Kelly

Anonymity. Invisibility. The lot of women over sixty and any man who works in coveralls. The first name embroidered on a faded, breast-pocket panel is less likely to be Remington, Bryce or Sterling than Ed, Ace or Buddy. If a passerby notices anything at all about this particular work site, it is probably the big, yellow digger, rather than the four workers in gray coveralls and hard hats.

The man controlling the joystick in the open-air cab of the Bobcat Tuff-Lift excavator drops the bucket down for another fifteen-inch wide chomp into the grass of the suburban park. The trench must accommodate pipes with an outside diameter of thirty-six inches, so forward momentum is slow, giving ample time for the two guys setting up the flexible fencing panels on either side of the dig track to stay ahead of the Bobcat's progress.

The mesh tape sections are flimsy enough to be supported by slender, bamboo rods at eight-foot intervals, and could easily be breached by a determined Yorkie-Poo, but their day-glow orange color and attached DANGER signs deter nosy-parkers from stepping too close to the trench.

By lunchtime, the crew has dug out three-quarters of the needed hundred-foot length, leaving more than enough daylight to complete the excavating, drop in the pipes, and backfill with the removed dirt by quitting time. The two fencers cross the street to a little mom and pop café for their break, while the foreman and the Bobcat operator tote manly metal lunch pails to a nearby park bench where they can eat their sandwiches and keep an eye on the site.

An hour into the afternoon's work, the digger reaches the terminus of the excavation: a sidewalk that rings the park. A quick swap of the bucket for a chain-rig that will hoist the lengths of stacked, corrugated pipe, and three of the men start on phase two of the day's job. The foreman remains on the sidewalk at the open end of the trench.

A uniformed cop, one of three young officers assigned by the city to do neighborhood public relations and community outreach, wanders over to the foreman on his once-a-day perambulation around the park's perimeter. For Officer Sanderson, the leisurely stroll normally involves only waves to joggers, and friendly hellos to nannies and young moms exposing their tiny charges to a dose of vitamin D. He carries lollipops in his pocket, the round ones with looped handles that ensure no tot pokes out his or her eye while enjoying a hit of straight sugar.

"What we got going on here," Sanderson asks amiably, while sucking on a cherry-flavored Safety Pop.

"Natural gas line extension," the foreman responds.

Sanderson notes the size of the pipe section being lowered into the freshly dug trench with the manual assistance of the two men not sitting in the Bobcat's cab.

"Damn. I never knew those things were so huge."

"Oh, that's just the protective housing. Gas pipe itself is only about yay big," the foreman responds, using both hands to form a roundish opening approximately seven inches wide.

"Huh. I learn something new every day."

"That's because you're so young. Old guy like me, I *forget* something every day."

Officer Sanderson chuckles and says, "Then I guess we balance each other out, don't we?" He glances at the sewn-on name tag to personalize the interaction, as he has been trained to do. "Well, Joe, you have a productive day."

Once the policeman strolls away, the foreman's tense shoulder muscles relax. He makes brief eye contact with the man operating the Bobcat, giving a subtle nod to assure him everything is copacetic.

By 4:30, the pipe is buried, the trench is backfilled, and the site is ready for a turf crew to lay sod the next morning.

So ends Monday of the work week.

A large, rough-looking flatbed truck backs in close to the covered trench, decanting four men in khaki coveralls who begin offloading pallets piled high with sod squares. The stitched pocket panel of the man who was Joe yesterday, now reads Eli. Without the grizzled sideburns sticking out from under his hard hat, and the thick, gray mustache, he appears to be twenty years younger than "Joe," closer to his own real age of thirty-one, but, on the off chance the same cop meanders by during the turf installation, Eli has switched places with his brother. Yesterday's Bobcat operator has been bumped up to foreman, his new name tag reading Chuck.

Officer Sanderson wanders past the worksite mid-afternoon, and is impressed by how quickly the plowed strip is reverting to its previous condition. With the exception of some faint lines between the two-foot-squares of grass, the covered area over the gas line extension already blends in with the rest of the park grounds.

Because he wants to wrap his shift on the dot, so as not to be late for his Tuesday night bowling league, the rookie officer doesn't stop to chat with the man supervising the movements of the other three. Instead, he removes the grape lolly from his mouth only long enough to acknowledge the crew with a smile and a Miss America-style wave.

The beer-bellied foreman with the bushy, red beard answers the casual greeting with a touch of his fingertips to the edge of his hard hat, then turns back to supervise the last few yards of sod installation.

By 4:30, all turf squares are in place and Chuck pays his pair of laborers the agreed-upon amount for two days' work, in cash, plus an extra fifty on top for each man. It's a small price for their requested silence about the job, reinforced with the dangled (though bogus) promise of more well-paid work over the coming months. After the two locals take off, Eli unscrews the back panel of the nearest public drinking fountain while Chuck drags over the heavy, industrial hose and hooks it up to the municipal water source.

The brothers have done this before. They know a good soaking will coax the roots of the sod to catch almost overnight, allowing the surface blades of grass to relax and obscure those faint lines of demarcation before the end of the week, which is why they spend ninety minutes drenching their handiwork. By 6:15, the hose has been disconnected, the water fountain put back into normal usage, and the mesh panels loaded onto the flatbed, so the brothers are ready to grab a bag of drive-through burgers and head back to their motel on the outskirts of the city.

The one who is currently Chuck unsnaps the top of his coveralls to remove the uncomfortable pregnancy belly simulator. His red beard will have to wait till he gets back to their room and can remove it with special solvent. The one who is currently Eli fires up the engine of the big truck that has one more job to do tomorrow before joining the Bobcat inside an abandoned barn an hour's drive away.

So ends Tuesday of the work week.

When the sleek, black Lincoln glides to a stop in front of Wee Precious Pre-School five minutes earlier than normal, Miss Mandy hurries to take Winston Haverty's pudgy, dimpled hand in hers to walk him through the open door and out to his ride.

Today that ride is the stretch limousine, so Mandy feels a moment of disappointment. When the Havertys send their Town Car, she uses those moments strapping Winston into his Scandinavian-made kiddie seat as an opportunity to flirt with Trevor, the family's main driver, whose rakish grin, tossed over his right shoulder from the driver's seat, always stirs a flutter in the young woman's chest.

The darkly tinted windows of the stretch limo, along with the opaque privacy panel between the front seats and the passenger cabin, prevent the pretty teacher's aide from identifying who's behind the wheel, so she remains strictly professional while securing her three-year-old charge into the pricey throne comprised of high-impact plastic and a daunting web of inch-wide, padded straps. She doesn't risk a smile at the blank expanse of the closed panel, lest she inadvertently encourage the Havertys' *second* driver, Gabe, a man twice her age who has, on several occasions, telegraphed his interest in her by creepily staring at her breasts in the rear view mirror while she leaned into the back to truss-up Winston.

As always, she pulls a chilled juice box from the pocket of her smock and, as always, Winston eagerly holds out both hands for his treat.

"Orn chooss," he demands, kicking his Lucchese-booted feet in anticipation, while Mandy tears off the seal and inserts the miniature straw.

Once he gets both hands wrapped around the box and the straw between his lips, Winston's five-day-a-week caretaker smooches the tip of her index finger and taps it on the end of his button nose with a "boop" sound, before closing the limousine door. Not all her kids at Wee Precious receive this platinum-level service, but the diamond tennis bracelet on Mandy's slender wrist speaks volumes about Winston's mother's transactional generosity in exchange for the assurance her princeling is treated with the deference she believes is his birthright.

Making her usual knuckle-tap on the right, rear window, Mandy signals the driver that Winston is set for his trip home. The stretch smoothly navigates the right curve of the wide, circular drive of the prestigious academy for monied moppets, then turns onto the tree-lined road leading away.

Ten minutes later, as Amanda Charles places scattered toys back on shelves, and returns left-behind personal items to the dedicated cubbies of their diminutive owners, Miss Carol steps into the doorway with a conspiratorial grin on her face.

"Your boo is here," she says, a teasing lilt to her words.

Mandy turns to scan the room for something Winston might have left behind, as well as to hide her blushing. Everyone at Wee Presh knows she has feelings for the handsome chauffeur employed by the Havertys, but only from observation, not from anything she has ever admitted to in the break room or outside of work.

Finding no toy, blankie or article of designer clothing that might have prompted the driver's quick return, Mandy walks to the lobby where Trevor waits, his cap respectfully removed and held in both hands. Considerate gestures like this make him even more attractive than his genetics already did.

"Sorry I'm late, Miss Mandy, but an old truck stalled out on Clayton Way, so I got boxed in for a few minutes."

Mandy glances over the braided epaulet on his left shoulder and sees the Lincoln Town Car idling out front, suddenly understanding what must have happened.

"Oh, Trevor, I think there's been a mix-up. Gabe already came for Winston in the stretch."

The chauffeur's eyebrows nearly touch, as confusion registers on his damn-near-perfect face.

"No, Gabe's driving Mr. H to the airport to meet a client flying in from Japan. I saw them pull away an hour ago."

His intense brown eyes lock with her pellucid blue ones, as they simultaneously realize both little Winston *and* their jobs may be in grave danger. The blood that has so recently pinked Mandy's cheeks drains from her face. Her knees give way, and Trevor leaps forward to catch her.

Sadly, the fainter is already out cold when the uniformed hottie scoops her up in his muscular arms and, in a move worthy of the cover of a romance novel, strides over to the huge couch with her snugged against his chest. The rest of the staff watches as he gently places their colleague down onto the burgundy suede cushions. Sighs are consciously suppressed.

So ends Wednesday of the work week.

The FBI profiler flown in to assist the local constabulary with the kidnapping is on his way from the airport to the Havertys' home, where Lt. Avery Florenda briefs a team of detectives in his temporary situation room. A dozen forensic technicians and photographers document every fingerprint and potential clue in the sprawling mansion.

As soon as Enid, a member of the housekeeping staff, announced her discovery of a ransom note in with the mail she dutifully bought in and began sorting through the afternoon before, Brian Haverty called the chief of police directly and the chief ordered Lt. Florenda to scramble a team. Only in movies are wealthy parents gullible enough to trust the word of a scumbag promising the safe return of their offspring in exchange for money. The very fact the kidnapper is willing to traumatize a toddler with capture and captivity undercuts any assurance he intends to honor the terms of the agreement.

The demand note is not comprised of colorful letters snipped from the few remaining paper magazines, but typed, apparently on an ancient, manual typewriter from the looks of the raggedy-ass, not-quite-lined-up letters. Curiously, it is a copy, rather than the original.

Here are the terms for the safe return of you're kid:
1. $200,000 in equal numbers of hundreds, fifties and twenties in a white kitchen garbage bag
2. If more than 5 bills are consecutive, he dies
3. If any tracking devise is with the cash, he dies
4. If a dye pack is with the cash, he dies
5. If you call the cops, he dies

Drop the bag with the cash into the trash can nearest the south entrance of Bennet Park tomorrow at noon. Drive you're own car and park just long enough to put the bag in the can. I will be watching, so come alone. After I see you drive away, I will take the money to where I can count it and check for any funny stuff. If everything is fine, I will tell you at 5 o'clock where to pick up you're kid. He will be safe as long as you don't pull any stupid stunts with the money.

Lt. Florenda wonders aloud why the kidnapper would name a drop-point so early in the game. The usual criminal M.O. is to issue instructions at the last minute, preventing law enforcement from setting up lookouts and plainclothes officers in advance.

"Because he's stupid?" suggests Det. Wong.

"Maybe. Or maybe this is his first rodeo. He might not realize the advantage he's giving us."

"I vote with Wong on stupid," says Det. Bledsoe. "The note gives away that he's working alone, which defies common sense."

Every cop in the room knows there's risk in grabbing the pick-up guy if he has partners. As soon as the other kidnappers know the drop is queered, they have no incentive to do anything but flee, so their hostage is suddenly dead-weight at best, or—in the worst-case scenario—a witness. No reason to keep a potential witness alive, especially if they'll slow the getaway.

"You both assume he's telling the truth about working alone. I don't think he's stupid."

Florenda goes on to point out the precise instructions about the ransom, each one making it harder to trace the cash and easier to spend it.

"Not to mention the fact that the note is a photocopy. No chance of forensics tracing the typewriter ribbon or paper," claims the lieutenant. "I guarantee the copy itself will be the most common, generic, 20-pound bond in the country."

His next point is the kidnapper's seemingly deliberate attempt to appear dumb by misspelling *your*, *device* and *entrance*, when he manages to get a much more difficult word—consecutive—correct.

"Moving on from the guy's IQ, do we like any of the Havertys' employees so far?"

"The older driver has a sheet," volunteers Cheryl Kane, the young detective assigned to interviewing the staff. "Mostly thirty-year-old juvie stuff involving joy rides and peddling weed to middle-schoolers when he was in high school, but a couple more recent for bar fights and check-kiting."

"How'd a puke like that score a sweet gig like this one?"

Kane looks around to see if anyone else knows. Shrugs and blank stares, so she goes on, providing information she learned from her father the night before. He'd been a year behind Gabe Dean and Brian Haverty at school and said they were close enough friends that the successful businessman had a long history of throwing the occasional bone to his old bud. Loans, references and, about six months ago, the backup chauffeur gig.

Upon arrival, the profiler offers his own thoughts about the kidnapper.

"Forties, blue-collar," Special Agent Virgil Dance announces confidently. "Unemployed or under-employed. That's why he's forced to take this desperate risk to get money, and is likely to make a mistake."

He opines the kidnapper has an elderly parent to take care of, or maybe medical bills for a chronically ill child. Or possibly a foreclosure that needs to be stopped.

Florenda listens with a look of interest on his face, but, in the lieutenant's experience, these guys are about as accurate as a TV psychic.

Has anyone in the auditorium lost a loved one? I have a person coming through with the letter "e" in their name. Could be a "c." Or maybe I'm sensing a beloved pet.

Once the fed's nebulous analysis comes to an end, he begs off to go to his hotel and freshen up, while Florenda calls for second interviews with the Disney-Prince driver and the pre-school teacher.

"The Havertys have confirmed their generosity in rewarding good service. Hence, the limo jockey's Rolex watch and the sparkly bracelet on Teach's wrist."

Det. Kane had privately confided to him her radar was picking up a romantic connection between the two, so Florenda surmises they might have gotten tired of waiting for the trickle-down economics of the Havertys' munificence, and gone for a bigger, faster score.

"Bledsoe, look for any indication they were planning to take off together sometime soon. Plane tickets to Rio, that sort of thing."

"Will do, Lieutenant."

"And, Wong, dive deeper into that older driver. Known criminal associates, recent movements; you know the drill."

"On it."

While detectives scatter to cover their assigned bases, Florenda meets again with the Havertys in their kitchen, where the missus stays busy making pots of coffee and simple sandwiches for the officers who spent the night in her home, searching for clues and interviewing staff. It keeps her tears at bay and, with every maid and cook under suspicion, forces her to become reacquainted with her kitchen appliances.

As Barbara Haverty putters, her husband Brian makes calls to three bankers, ensuring the specific denominations and quantities of the ransom bills will be delivered to the house by ten tomorrow morning.

Late in the evening, Lt. Avery Florenda checks in with HQ to verify the park is set to be blanketed with official watchers, in the guise of joggers, the homeless, and trash-stabbing groundskeepers, long before the noon go-time. The chief of police has specifically told him not to request snipers for the overlooking roof tops, so he confirms the officers up there will be armed only with binoculars. The goal is to follow the kidnapper to wherever little Winston is being held, not to arrest him at the pickup.

"Have you arranged for a couple female officers to pose as mothers with strollers near the drop site," he asks the person on the phone. After listening to their answer, he says, "Good. And make sure those baby dolls look real enough to fool our perp if he decides to wander past them on his way to the cash."

So ends Thursday of the work week.

Because the family is *very* influential, both socially and politically, the chief of police has personally authorized a five-hour buyout of all the seats in Café Delicioso, a mom and pop eatery directly across the street from the ransom drop. A swift, positive outcome on the kidnapping guarantees the chief's future run for district attorney will have numerous, wealthy donors.

The coffee at Delicioso is excellent, but as the café's only customer, Lt. Avery Florenda, brings the fifth cup of the day to his lips, he tastes only bitterness. It is after four and no one has come for the ransom money. He has been in constant communication with the teams watching the park, since the moment Brian Haverty pulled up to the designated trash can at one minute to noon and stopped his Land Rover long enough to place the garbage bag stuffed with currency into the open mesh receptacle sitting alongside the sidewalk.

By now, after staring at the pickup spot for hours through a pair of binoculars, Avery feels he knows every square inch of the damned thing: the gray metal, diamond-pattern mesh; the folded-over top of the black plastic bin liner; the strap that secures the folded-over strip to the rim, preventing the liner from getting dragged down inside the can when some idiot discards a heavy object.

The frustrated lieutenant is correct in his belief he now possesses intimate knowledge of that particular can, but, since the rest of them along the sidewalk circling the park are spaced at sixty-foot intervals, he has not had an opportunity to compare this one with the others. If he had, an observant cop like Avery Florenda would have noticed several inconsistencies.

He reluctantly calls for the operation to shut down, assuming the kidnapper must have whiffed to the police presence. He hopes this doesn't jeopardize little Winston's chance of survival and that his captor will risk another play for the cash.

Florenda thanks the married couple that runs Delicioso, tells them they can flip over the Open sign, then exits.

Across the street, a rookie officer approaches the bin to retrieve the white garbage bag. He's been elected because nobody senior to him wants to pick through all the nasty stuff tossed on top of the ransom money during the long afternoon's wait: the dripping remains of a child's dropped ice-cream cone, a half-full, one-liter Dr Pepper, a loaded diaper one of the nannies didn't want to carry home after changing a baby she should *not* have let eat some of the grass it crawled on.

The rookie bends over the can, looks inside, then immediately shouts, "It's empty!"

Avery Florenda runs across the street, getting to the can the same time as half a dozen plainclothes officers. One glance confirms the rookie's claim, and Avery grabs the plastic liner, pulling it inside out and yanking it free of the belt that has held it snugly to the wire mesh. The bottom has been neatly cut out, and, as he thrusts the liner into the hands of the nearest detective, he barks, "Evidence bag! Now!"

Leaning over the rim of the can, the lieutenant looks through its open bottom into a hole littered with remnants of the afternoon's offerings: a now-empty Dr Pepper bottle, a stinky, leaking Pampers, and the soggy, collapsed cone of a child's ice cream treat. He tries to push the trash can aside to get a better look into the hole, but the can doesn't budge. It is not until he and Det. Bledsoe lift it straight up that it pulls free from its moorings: three sturdy rods soldered onto the bottom, aftermarket skewers designed to hold the can securely in place.

The smallest female officer is kitted-out with a head-to-toe, white paper jump suit—the kind forensics guys call *hazmat lite*—before she sits on the grass at the edge of the opening and lowers herself down. The drop is so short that Officer Penn's head and shoulders are still above ground when her bootied feet touch bottom. Scrunching over, she finds a large, vertical opening in the side of the hole.

"Hand me a flashlight," she says, popping up like an albino meerkat. "It looks like there's some kind of tunnel."

When Florenda sees where Officer Penn aims her beam, he scans the ground in that direction. Using his shoe to sweep aside the grass blades, he notices a faint demarcation line, then bends to examine it more closely.

"This is fresh sod," he announces, yanking up a square for proof. Now that he knows it's here, his eyes pick up the track and he follows it. "Officer Penn," he calls out over his shoulder. "Proceed with caution down the tunnel."

He follows the track above, while Regina Penn crawls through the corrugated pipe. Some of the detectives join the lieutenant, while others hover near the hole by the sidewalk.

The sod trail dead-ends at a knee-high, rectangular structure bearing the ominous, stenciled warning: DANGER – HIGH VOLTAGE. The words are reinforced with a scary lightning bolt, but Avery Florenda is no fool. He's certain truly dangerous power equipment would be housed in something sturdier than the four-foot by three-foot plywood box on the ground. Double-checking that the path does not pick up on the other side, the lieutenant easily lifts off the dummy cover.

Looking down, he sees the inert figure of Winston Haverty, curled up in a collapsible playpen, surrounded by stuffed animals, juice boxes and the remnants of a PB&J on a paper plate. Before Avery can shout for medical help, Officer Penn gets to the boy from the tunnel. Reaching over the mesh side of the playpen, she lays fingers on his carotid and yells up, "He's alive!"

The noise wakes the child, who sleepily allows the goggled, white creature to lift him up toward the man leaning over the opening. As Lt. Florenda slips his hands under the child's arms to hoist him out, Winston utters the only words he will ever say about the incident that will remain forever unsolved.

"Orn chooss?"

So ends Friday of the work week.

With their razor-cut dark hair and Italian-cut dark suits, the two men striding down concourse A to gate 11 this Saturday morning look every inch the Wall Street wolf cubs. Or maybe charismatic sellers of multi-million-dollar yachts. Each is closely trailed by a Swaine Adeney Brigg rolling bag, the same one King Charles uses when he flies, although His Majesty's socks and unmentionables are, presumably, packed by a valet rather than his own hands. Like all who travel for business, the brothers look forward to returning home after the completion of their lucrative out-of-town project.

The gate agent who scans their boarding passes appraises them with a subtle once-over, wondering why *he* can't find a partner so obviously successful and pulled-together. It would shock him to learn they are *not* Ivy League educated trust fund babies, but self-made men.

Several minutes later, a flight attendant offers them glasses of pre-flight champagne, but Logan, at twenty-nine the younger of the pair, flashes her a charming smile, all dimples and straight, white teeth, saying, "Sadly, I'm not old enough to drink, and my big brother has to work." Even the wink he gives her to signal he's joking comes across as adorably playful, unlike the overt, creepy ones she so often gets from rich, entitled men who fly first class.

James, thirty-one, speaks to Keri—for that is the name on the flight attendant's plastic name tag—long enough to order two bottled waters. His tone is much more serious than his brother's, but one hundred percent respectful, and the young woman hurries away to fulfill the drink order of the memorable gentlemen in 3-C and 3-D.

Setting the miniature water bottles and glasses of ice on their separate tray tables, Keri is surprised to see the tablet the serious one has pulled out of his carry-on is an old-style, lined yellow pad. She would have expected him to own the latest cutting-edge tech, but if there is one thing the Maris siblings know, it is that tech equals traceability. The only time they use computers in setting up their operations is in the initial scouting phase.

That's when they find financially strapped farmers, not too far from their target, willing to lease a hundred acres or so to a private hunter. The farmer never knows the appeal of his land is not deer or rabbits, but the presence of a barn suitable for temporarily stashing a few large pieces of equipment and whatever disguises and "uniforms" the job will require. All he cares about is the substantial sum he receives up front for a six-month lease on land he isn't using anyway.

Once the brothers have all the necessary local maps and newspaper articles about their chosen city's wealthiest families, they go old school for a final week of recon from a low-end motel. They've done the tunnel caper enough times to net close to a million dollars. And since they had already decided Winston Haverty would be the last tot they would host overnight—just in case some national database begins to notice a pattern in the kidnappings—James enters expenses by hand to get an accurate accounting of their ultimate take.

He amortizes the purchase of the Bobcat over five uses, calculates its value at a low enough price to guarantee a quick sale, than does the math. Scribbling a bottom-line number, he circles it with a flourish of his gold MontBlanc Meisterstück, then nudges his brother and passes him the yellow pad.

Logan scans the columns of figures, eventually asking, "So, we're keeping the truck?"

"For now. Depends on what we come up with next."

The Maris boys have been pulling off remarkable thefts since they were teenagers fresh out of foster care and working minimum-wage jobs in grease-stained coveralls. Their early attempts only provided basic survival, but over the past decade, they have perfected their craft, tweaking each imaginative way to separate rich people from a small portion of their money in a manner that eliminates all risk of getting caught, while providing them with a luxury lifestyle they could only dream of as boys.

Neither Logan, nor James, knows yet the parameters of their next larcenous venture, but the brothers understand it will be accomplished, as always, by utilizing their cloaks of invisibility: worn coveralls with pocket patches identifying the wearer as a Hank, a T.J. or an Al.

THE OBSOLETE

Richard Hallows

"You don't see many pawn shops around anymore, do you?" It was part question and part statement of fact, as the detective picked up an interesting piece of Clarence Cliff pottery: a teapot with an angular handle like a schoolboy's set square. "Is this worth anything?" he asked.

"Three grand," I told him.

"For a tea pot?" He stared at it and gently placed it back on the table from which he had taken it. "You've got to drink a lot of tea to justify a three grand tea pot." The detective smiled and displayed his expensive dental work. You had to work a lot of extra shifts to afford teeth like that.

I smiled in agreement. If I had acquired any wisdom with age it was that the less said at times like this, the better.

"People collect them," I told him.

"What kind of people?" he asked.

I shrugged.

"People who collect tea pots, I guess."

"Did you buy it?" he asked.

"House clearance, I think."

"Somebody didn't bring it in to the shop to sell it to you?"

"No. Fairly sure it was a house clearance. eBay and Facebook have pretty much put an end to walk-ins. Everyone thinks they can get rich buying and selling on the Internet."

"Times change," said the detective. He glanced at his watch as if checking that times really did change. I wondered if anyone ever asked him how he afforded a ten grand Rolex.

"Tell me about it," I said. "There's no respect for the past."

"I know. It's all 'cyber this' and 'cyber that.' Nobody chases criminals anymore; they just trace IP addresses. Good old-fashioned coppering is obsolete now."

I nodded as if I knew what he was talking about. The detective was, as I was, of the old school, right down to the rubber soled brown brogues, grey overcoat, and matching homburg. He was, the epitome of a gumshoe, only more expensively accessorised.

"You've got plenty of stock though." He gestured at the packed shelves.

"Such as it is," I said. "Nobody's going to get rich selling nineteen fifties tea pots. They're obsolete too."

"And yet here you are," said the detective.

"Old school," I told him.

There was no money in most of it anymore, but every now and then, something worthwhile would come along. In my case it was nine hundred and seventy-two uncut diamonds. Relatively easy to move at the right time, completely untraceable, and worth at least thirty million.

He was silent as he continued his inspection of the contents of the shop. I hoped he didn't have anything in particular he was hoping to find. Diamonds, for example. eBay and Facebook had done one good thing for me, which was to provide another option for the type of criminals none of us liked to deal with. If you were dealing with professionals, you could have a certain amount of confidence in the quality of the merchandise, and, more importantly, that there was no danger of being called as a witness in a murder trial or finding your stock featured as part of a 'House of Horror' story on the front page of the tabloids. It was the unprofessional chancers who had migrated their operation online. They had never really understood the role of a good fence. The decent crooks still liked to deal with people, and they knew that a good fence did more than just sell the goods. We are a barrier between the secretive act of stealing and the necessarily more public act of converting stolen goods into cash. I was once described as a condom for stolen goods, which sounds insulting, but actually shows I prevent all kinds of potential problems.

I followed the detective as he walked towards the back of the store.

"You seen Freddie the Frog recently?" He turned towards me to watch my response.

"That's a name I haven't heard for a long time." I tried to sound as if I was telling the truth and wondered if the detective was wearing a wire.

"Why do they call him that?"

"Call him what?"

"The Frog."

"Just the alliteration, I guess." I thought for a moment. "And his strange leaping capability."

"Leaping capability?"

"Oh, he could jump ten feet from a standing start. I once saw him jump from a window to the wall of another building and just hold himself there."

"Sounds more like Spiderman."

"Freddie the Spider doesn't really have the right ring to it though, does it?" I said.

The detective grunted in grudging agreement.

"Have you seen the tree frogs on that David Attenborough documentary?" I asked.

The detective shook his head.

"Weird little bright green things with bug eyes that jump for miles. Well that was what he was like."

"A weird little green thing with bug eyes?" The detective squeezed the end of his nose between his thumb and forefinger. It was a strange gesture. "You're sure it's not just because he's as mad as a box of?"

"A box of what?"

"Frogs."

I thought about it for a moment.

"Is he mad?" I asked.

"As a box of frogs," said the detective, authoritatively.

"He was alright the last time I saw him," I said.

"When was that?"

"Must have been a year ago."

"That was before his breakdown." The detective smiled as if mental illness was something to be pleased about.

"I didn't know he'd had a breakdown."

"It was probably the stress of witness protection."

"Now, I didn't know he was in witness protection either."

"We'll he isn't any more. He stopped cooperating—right after the breakdown."

"So, you've lost him?"

"Yep."

"And he's insane?"

"Insane might be a little harsh, but yes, basically a box of frogs." The detective smiled and it looked as if the light glinted off his front teeth.

"And you think I know where he is?"

"We thought he might be here."

"Why?"

"Because the last thing he wrote in his own excrement on the wall of his safe house was that he was going to kill you."

"You probably could have led with that if you'd wanted my attention."

"I like to build up to a punch line." The detective smiled again. It occurred to me that he smiled a lot for a man without much to smile about.

The fact that Freddie the Frog wrote the message on the wall in his own faeces showed more commitment than I had expected. He could have just left a note like anyone else.

"Anyway," continued the detective, "I thought I'd better let you know there's a crazed killer out hunting you."

"So, are you offering me protection?" I asked.

"What? A lot of love and affection?" The detective was a Robbie Williams fan.

"I was thinking more about twenty-four-hour surveillance."

"We've had you under covert surveillance for a while," said the detective.

"I hadn't noticed," I said.

"That's why they call it covert." The detective smiled again. He glanced round the room as if something had changed in the past few moments. He pursed his lips, shook his head, and finally thrust his hands into his overcoat pockets with an air of finality and walk towards the door.

"I'll be seeing you," he said as he pushed the door.

"It's pull," I told him.

The detective scowled and pulled the door open.

He drifted across the road to the unmarked car that pulled up. He leaned down to speak into the driver's window and when he had finished the car drove away.

"I guess that's a no to protection then," I muttered.

"That's a shame," said a voice from behind me. "And just when you needed it most."

"How are you, Freddie?" I said without needing to turn around.

"I've been worse," he said.

I turned around.

"It's good to see you," said Freddie. He smiled and took a step forward with his arms outstretched. "I'm a hugger," he said.

"When did that happen?" I stepped, uncomfortably, into his embrace.

"You get into the habit when you're checking everyone you meet for a wire."

I felt him pat my sides. It could have been a gesture of affection, but it wasn't.

"Why would I wear a wire?" I asked.

"You never know," said Freddie.

'Like you never know a bent copper until it's too late?" It was a rhetorical question.

"I know. I know. You told me so," said Freddie.

"Damn," I said. "I wanted to say that."

"How did you know?"

I wanted to say something vague like 'intuition,' but it wasn't really intuition, it was forty years of being a fence. After a while you can read people. You can't make a living at it without being able to do that. If you're not in the business you make the mistake of thinking it's about knowing about the stuff they want to sell, but most of the time it's more about understanding the people who want to sell it. As with most things in life, there are degrees of dishonesty. You can be a thief and still be trusted. In fact, I would go further than that; you can't be a professional thief without being trustworthy. I had always known the detective was on the take.

"Teeth," I told him.

"Teeth?"

"His teeth are too good. When I first met him he had a smile like an old piano: black and white with bits missing. Now, he could be used to advertise toothpaste."

"I just thought he had a nice smile," said Freddie.

"He should. It probably cost north of thirty grand. And you don't spend that on a coppers' salary."

Freddie was silent.

"And you can add to that, an expensive taste in custom shoes, a gold Oyster on his left wrist and that stupid hat he's been wearing since he started his hair transplant treatment."

"And that makes you think he's on the take?" It felt as if this was old news to Freddie.

"He's either on the take or he's won the lottery, and of he'd won the lottery he wouldn't be working anymore."

"You should be on TV," said Freddie. "You'd make a fortune."

"I've not got the legs for it," I said.

"Very true," he agreed.

"But more important than that is what we are going to do about this crook. He's everything that's wrong with the world today."

"I know lots of people who would kill him for less than the price of that tea pot," said Freddie. "You meet all sorts in genpop these days."

"I was thinking more by way of an anonymous tip off."

Freddie looked disappointed.

"Where's the fun in that?" he asked. "We should have him killed."

"Well, a phone call is a lot cheaper, and probably not as messy," I argued.

"A bit anti-climactic, don't you think?" said Freddie. "It doesn't have the drama of a protracted death scene."

"More realistic though," I said. "And if you're a fence the last thing you want is drama."

"I suppose," said Freddie. "But have we got anything we can use as evidence?"

"We don't need evidence. We just need to start the investigation. The police will find the evidence."

"And we do nothing?" If it was possible, Freddie looked more disappointed.

"There are no heroics involved in being a fence," I told him. "If anything, it's the opposite."

I took an old Nokia out of a drawer.

"Police," I said when a young voice asked which service I required. "A man is trying to kill me. He's got a gun," I added as I reached down into the desk drawer and took out the old Smith & Wesson I kept there. It was an ugly little snub nosed hammerless revolver, designed for the less discrete close-up killer, or anyone who wants to put a thirty-eight calibre round into someone at close range. It was a favourite for bedside cabinets and inside jacket pockets alike and had come to me as part of a job lot from a string of high-profile burglaries.

Freddie's face went from disappointed to confused. I smiled. It must have been contagious.

"Why?" asked Freddie.

"Because you told him."

"Told him what?"

"About the diamonds."

Freddie was silent for a moment.

"Why would I do that?" he asked.

"Well, let me think. It can't have been a lot of fun in genpop. He got you out of prison and into witness protection. He's not going to do that for nothing is he?"

I paused and tried to judge whether I was on the right track. A slight twitch beneath Freddie's left eye suggested I was.

"So, what was the plan?" I asked. "Because I can't see any way that this ends well for you."

"It was simple really," said Freddie. "I kill you, take the diamonds, give him ninety per cent of them and he gives me a plane ticket to somewhere warm without an extradition treaty."

"Well, when you put it that way," I said. "It still sounds ridiculous."

Freddie looked towards the door as if thinking about trying to escape.

"How about this instead?"

"What?" Freddie was right to be worried.

"You come in here trying to rob the store. I shoot you and the detective arrives just in time to be a key witness to an act of self-defence. I give him half the diamonds and don't have to get on a plane to anywhere."

"Why would he double cross me like that?" Freddie was more confused than ever.

"Think about it. You've done your part of the job by stealing the diamonds. The only thing left is to sell them on. We're all obsolete, but right now, you're more obsolete than the rest of us."

EXODUS

Jillian Grant Shoichet

Edith Zuckerman was a stickler for verisimilitude, and in many ways, this Passover night was not so different from all other nights.

But on this night, unbeknownst to Edith's guests, the blood on the Zuckerman front door jamb was not kosher, the roasted shank bone on the Seder plate was not lamb, and Herb Zuckerman was not "held up at the office."

When they were growing up, the Zuckermans were the only kids at Toronto's Forest Hill Collegiate whose mother lit real oil lamps at Hannukah. She lined the glass bulbs along the front window behind the sofa. She used only kosher cold-pressed virgin olive oil from Israel. On the eighth day of the Festival of Lights, by which time both the bulbs and the windowpanes were an opaque, smoky grey, Edith Zuckerman would tell Maria to clean the glass and phone Sears to book the Zuckermans' annual upholstery and carpet steaming appointment.

During the harvest holiday of Sukkot, Maria was instructed to serve all three meals of each festival day in the backyard sukkah, the temporary pergola's ceiling of greenery festooned exuberantly with gourd and squash. Even when the temperature dipped below freezing. Even when it snowed.

But it was on Passover, the holiday that marked the end of 400 years of slavery and the Jews' Exodus from Egypt, that Edith truly shone. One memorable Passover past, on Edith's instruction, the gardener released a vanload of frogs into the front yard (Plague Two of the ten plagues of Moses). For the next few weeks, frogs plagued Forest Hill, appearing in planters and fountains and swimming pools and—once—a martini glass. Another year, in the spirit of verisimilitude, Edith had Maria treat all four Zuckerman children for head lice (Plague Three), despite the fact that none of them actually had lice. Then there was the year she insisted the entire first meal of Passover be conducted without light (Plague Nine, when darkness fell upon the land of Egypt). That year, Herb Zuckerman put his foot down: he couldn't very well lead an entire Seder service in the dark.

Edith allowed him an adjustable mini book light.

There was no boxed Manischewitz matzah in the Zuckerman household at

Passover. All the unleavened bread for the eight-day festival—lunchbox staple for the week—was baked in the Zuckerman kitchen by Maria, the longest serving of the Zuckermans' Filipina maids. The irony of Maria's practically indentured servitude seemed lost on Edith—or perhaps she chalked it up to verisimilitude.

Each Passover, Edith had Maria swab the front door jamb with a liberal, Angel-of-Death-defying slick of real lamb's blood from the kosher butcher on Eglinton Avenue. Josh Zuckerman didn't know if his mother had ever contemplated a more drastic commemoration of Plague Ten—death of the Egyptian first-born—but he'd always been grateful he'd been born a Jew and not an Egyptian.

Still, this time of year made him anxious.

As he sat in his Mercedes in the bricked semi-circular drive of the Zuckerman family home, Josh Zuckerman took a deep, calming breath. It would be the first Passover that Elaine and the girls hadn't attended with him. The separation was still raw. He hadn't yet told his sister that Elaine had left; Rachel's sort of support was likely to make him feel worse. He'd informed his mother only last week—and only because he wanted to spare her the social embarrassment of three empty place settings at the table.

Headlights flashed in the rear view. His sister's elegant, spiderlike limbs unfurled themselves out the passenger door of Michael's Saab. Then the back of the car exploded, and three boys tumbled onto the driveway. A few moments later, Michael ejected himself out the driver's side door, his 240-pound frame still mostly muscle, though he now coached pro rugby rather than playing it. He tucked a boy under each arm and dribbled the third one up the front steps with his knees.

Josh lowered the window. Rachel bent towards him. Her perfume wafted across the front seat.

"She left, didn't she?"

He nodded.

"Oh, sweetheart." Her lips brushed his cheek. "She was an unforgiving, sanctimonious bitch. What does Mum always say? A woman of valour forgives minor transgressions. And *really*: You're a small-time college professor in a small-minded, inconsequential girls' prep school. Any sordid transgressions on *your* part hardly even qualify as *minor*, for goodness' sake. Elaine is certainly no woman of valour. She never was."

Josh was silent.

"Well, come on in. Let's get this over with."

"I'll be there in a minute."

He watched as she floated up the steps and disappeared through the front door.

Another flash of headlights, and two more cars pulled in behind the Saab: Jacob's Italian job and Ethan's Porsche. The two younger Zuckermans greeted each other warily. Then, to Josh's surprise, the passenger doors of both vehicles opened. From the Porsche stepped a statuesque blonde, fully four inches taller than Ethan himself. From the other vehicle clambered a short, dark-haired woman with glasses and a corduroy shoulder bag. Introductions were tendered and the unlikely foursome made its way up the front steps, passing the Mercedes without a sideways glance.

After a few moments, Josh unbuckled his seatbelt. He glanced briefly at the sky. The March night was cold and still. The skeletal branches of the old maple trees lining the sidewalk framed a full moon. Holiday candles flickered in the windows up and down the street (Easter and Passover coincided this year), and snatches of laughter and the scent of good, warm food punctuated the chilly air.

Josh sighed, mounted the steps, and pushed open the front door of the Zuckerman family home.

He was met at the door by a petite dark-eyed girl he didn't recognize. Petite dark-eyed girls came and went in the Zuckerman household. She bobbed her head appealingly and held out her hand for his coat.

He tucked his driving gloves into the pocket. "Where's Maria?"

The girl shrugged shyly. She was charming.

"I'm Josh. Josh Zuckerman."

The girl bobbed her head again.

"And you are?"

"Camilla."

"What a beautiful name." He flashed a Josh Zuckerman smile.

The girl blushed and shifted the leather overcoat and cashmere scarf to her other arm so she could take the hand he'd thrust towards her.

Josh squared his shoulders and entered the living room.

Jacob and Ethan had already raided Herb Zuckerman's liquor cabinet. Ethan held a gin and tonic in one hand, his other arm draped with nonchalant possessiveness across the back of a leather armchair occupied by the leggy blonde. The woman laughed at something Ethan said. She had very white teeth.

Jacob was pouring a drink for the bespectacled brunette, who still had her bag slung across her shoulder. Michael was sitting cross-legged on the floor playing a noisy game of Jenga with two of the boys. The youngest was pushing a replica logging truck along the Persian carpet. Rachel stood at the window that overlooked the wintry back garden, glass of wine in hand. Another newly planted tree stood slender and straight in the moonlight.

She turned when Josh entered the room, caught his eye, and nodded towards the kitchen—or, rather, the three-kitchens-in-one. Edith Zuckerman had a kitchen for meat meals, a kitchen for dairy, and a kitchen for Passover. Each kitchen had an oven, its own sink and dishwasher, and its own set of dishes. The Passover kitchen was sealed off from the rest of the house for all but eight days of every year—literally sealed off. At the end of the festival, Edith would supervise the cleaning and Saran-wrapping of all the appliances. The cupboards would be taped shut. Then the pocket doors would slide closed, the key would turn in the lock, and Passover would be over for another year.

But tonight, the far end of the kitchen was in full swing. A team of four Filipina women called directions to each other in Tagalog as one reduced the matzah balls to a simmer and another checked the brisket. In the middle of the bustle, exuding an air of dignified authority, was Edith Zuckerman.

As always, Josh was struck by how small his mother was in real life. Once, at McGill, a flatmate on a student exchange from South Asia had asked him to describe his mother. Josh struggled to paint an accurate picture. She was loving—or was it possessive? She was principled—or was it authoritarian? She was supportive—or was it domineering? Eventually, he lapsed into an awkward silence. He looked up to find the earnest young man staring at him with an unreadable expression.

"What?"

"She's like the goddess Kali."

"Who?"

"Kali, the protective destroyer. Your mother is Kali."

Josh had scoffed. The roommate shrugged and dropped the matter. Later, Josh had thumbed through a book of Hindu gods in the university library. Now, whenever he thought of Edith Zuckerman, he pictured her standing with one foot on his back, shaking her necklace of skulls, her ten terrible blue arms snaking out to snap the backs of her enemies.

"Darling!" Edith Zuckerman approached her eldest son with open arms and stood on tiptoe to receive his kiss on her cheek. "You're even later than Jacob—and he brought a *scholar,* of all things, with the most *extraordinary* taste in accessories. I was beginning to wonder if you would come at all, after what that horrible woman did to you right before the holidays. Over and over I've said to you boys, A true woman of valour finds a way to forgive minor transgressions. I *told* you to watch your step with her, darling. You wore the yellow one, I see." She tugged his tie straight, her opinion of the yellow one apparent.

"I like the yellow. I'm not late. You called it for 7:00." He didn't tell her he'd been sitting in the drive for twenty minutes before he got out of the car. He also didn't correct the Elaine timeline. What did it matter whether she'd left three months ago or three minutes ago?

"Did you get everyone a drink?"

"Not necessary. Jacob is playing gracious host. Where *is* Dad, by the way?"

Edith pursed her lips.

"I thought the whole idea of calling it for later was so he'd be here on time."

Edith said nothing.

Herb Zuckerman was a partner in a large corporate law firm. In Josh's memory, Herb had never been home for the start of the evening meal. Doubtless his memory was flawed, as all childhood memories are, but Herb Zuckerman was late frequently enough that being "held up at the office" had become the standard Zuckerman excuse for tardiness. Late for your 7:30 am basketball practice? That's because, Ethan announced airily to his coach, he'd been "held up at the office." Forgot to pick up your elder sibling from the airport? That's because, explained Rachel with a small smile, as Josh wrestled his carry-on into the trunk of the Saab, she'd been "held up at the office." The year they'd all failed to remember Edith's birthday, when Josh had frantically texted his younger siblings at 10:30 at night to *call your mother,* Edith had received four voice mail messages on her phone—all of them profuse and inadequate apologies for being "held up at the office."

"Well," said Josh tactfully, "everything *smells* wonderful."

"Of course it does, darling."

"Your kitchen is a well-oiled machine."

"Of course it is. Camilla, the soup is boiling over."

The lovely girl who had met him at the front door leapt across the kitchen.

"Where's Maria?" asked Josh. "I haven't seen her since December."

"That's what happens when you don't visit your mother. She's taken some holiday."

"At Passover? That's unusual."

"Are you questioning how your mother runs her household?"

Josh held up his hands. "Never. You're the queen. I'll get Jacob to pour me a drink."

He leaned down and kissed his mother again on the proffered cheek, then made his way back to the living room, a familiar foot-on-spine pressure between his shoulder blades.

Ten minutes later, the family was ushered into the formal dining room. It was Edith Zuckerman's tradition to keep the dining room doors firmly closed until the festive meal was about to begin—to encourage a fuller appreciation of the Lalique crystal and the gilt-edged place settings.

Silverware gleamed in the candlelight. The Seder plate, with its roasted shank bone, sat resplendent and smug in front of Herb Zuckerman's traditional seat at the head of the linen-shrouded table.

"It looks *lovely,* Mum," said Rachel.

"Of course it does, darling," said Edith.

The first hint that this night was not quite like other nights was when Edith Zuckerman took Herb's place at the head of the table.

"Oh, no," said Jacob in mock horror. "Dad's not held up at the office, is he?"

Edith smiled. "Not this time, darling. This year, *I* will be leading us out of Egypt."

In the brief silence that followed, Josh felt the pressure between his shoulder blades creep towards his neck. Rachel's eldest called from the foot of the table, "You *go,* Grandma!"

Edith smiled at her grandson and lifted her wine glass. "To family."

"To family," came the chorused reply.

As the Seder progressed, the ache at the base of Josh's skull moved upwards until it throbbed dully behind his eyes. The candles seemed to glow overly bright; the conversation around the table rose and fell as if someone was playing with the volume control. The red wine wasn't helping, but Camilla kept refilling his wine glass and he felt obliged to continue sipping.

When Rachel's youngest son—Nathan, wasn't it?—stood to ask the traditional Four Questions, Josh found himself asking the same thing: *Why is this night different from all other nights?* He looked at his mother, serene and untouchable at the head of the table. Her beatific smile embraced her children, her grandchildren, and her guests alike, bestowing upon the table a smothering mantle of holy bliss.

An idea began to gnaw at the corners of his mind. The idea persisted and, like his headache, began to grow. He was so distracted by it that he didn't hear the woman to his left, Jacob's near-sighted friend, ask him a question. When he looked up, both she and Jacob seemed to be waiting for his answer.

"Um, yes, I think so," he said, taking another sip of wine.

The woman raised an eyebrow. From his seat opposite, Jacob kicked Josh under the table. To his companion, he said, "Yes, he *does* have children. He has two daughters, who apparently now live with their mother." To his brother, Jacob mouthed the words "What's wrong with you?"

Josh didn't answer. His idea, at first so tentative and uncertain, now thudded relentlessly behind his eyes.

He cleared his throat.

Edith looked up. "Yes, darling?"

"I just wondered when Dad was coming home."

"I'm sure he won't be long now."

"He's not usually this late."

"Well, you know your father." Edith's voice was indulgent.

"Normally he leads the Seder service. On this night, we've got to the matzah balls and the gefilte fish and he still hasn't shown up." Even to his own ears, Josh's voice sounded plaintive.

Edith smiled gently. "I've been married to your father for a long time, darling. I've learned not to expect him to be here when I want him to be here. But we all forgive certain things in the people we love. We let things go. That's what Passover is all about."

"Is *that* what Passover's all about?" whispered Nathan loudly. "I thought it was about Exodus."

"*Exactly*," said Edith. "Passover *is* about Exodus. And Exodus is about letting go. Getting rid of people and things that pull us down. Breaking the chains of our past."

Josh drained the last mouthful of wine from his glass and leaned unsteadily to his right. In Rachel's ear he said, more loudly than he intended, "I think Dad made his own Exodus."

Conversation around the table ceased.

"Don't be ridiculous, Joshua," said Edith softly. "Why would your father do that?"

Josh scanned the table. Everyone was looking at him. The thudding behind his eyes now matched the hammering in his chest. He shoved his chair back and stood, flinging his arms outwards. "You tell me! Maybe he was having an affair with Maria! Maybe they escaped Egypt together!"

Edith arched a delicate eyebrow. "That's even more ridiculous. A husband has no need for escape if he has married a woman of valour. A woman of valour forgives the minor transgressions of her husband. Your *father* married a woman of valour. *Unlike his son.*"

Josh stared at his mother.

Edith took a measured sip of wine. "I told you. Maria has taken some time off." Her gentle smile took in the faces of her guests, the Seder plate and its roasted shank bone, the gilt-edged place settings, the crystal goblets—and the darkened window that overlooked the wintry back garden. With its newly planted tree. "Maria has needed rest for a very long time."

At that moment, the front door banged open and Herb's cheerful "Hello!" echoed through the house. A few seconds later, the jovial face of the head of the Zuckerman family appeared in the dining room door. "I'll be there in a minute—I just have to wash up. Edith, I couldn't find a single garden centre open this late on a Sunday. You've planted a lot of trees in that garden over the years. You've never needed me to run out for bone meal before. Why now? Why plant a tree today? Couldn't it have waited?"

He took two steps into the silent room and planted a kiss on the cheek that his wife tilted upwards.

Edith smiled fondly at him. "You're probably right. I'm sure the tree will be fine. The ground in that part of the garden is so naturally fertile. Go wash up. We were just talking about letting go of the past, breaking our chains of enslavement. You can join us."

REVERSION

Marcelle Dubé

Luke ran his hand over the top of the credenza he was sanding. It was a bigger piece than he was used to crafting and took up more of his woodworking shop—which used to be his stand-alone garage—than he liked, especially with the six chairs in various stages of completion stacked along one wall.

Even though the early October morning was chilly, he kept the garage doors open. He didn't want to be trapped inside with all that dust.

The wooden garage was old-fashioned, with double doors that had to be opened and closed by hand. It stood behind the house and to the side, at the end of a long, straight driveway that hugged the house. He parked his pickup in front of the garage and Annie parked her Bronco at the side of the house, near the wide spot, so he could get around her if he needed to.

He heard steps on the gravel outside and turned to see Annie walking around the pickup toward him in her no-nonsense navy slacks, flat shoes and red wool blazer. She came in and stood looking down at the credenza, her long, straight dark hair cascading down her back, her brown eyes lively with interest.

"It's looking good," she said.

Luke couldn't help it. He grinned. He was pretty sure approval from his wife was what kept his heart ticking.

"Thanks, honey. You off?"

She nodded and came over to bury herself in his arms, a warm bundle of plump curves and enticing scent. And now, dust.

"The kids will be sketching their favorite animals today." Her voice was muffled against his chest and he resisted the urge to kiss the top of her head. She didn't like that.

As if guessing his thought, she pulled away and smiled up at him.

"See you after school," she said.

He waved her off and watched her crunch over to her Bronco. He loved watching her walk.

Then he sighed and went back to sanding.

He had finished applying the first coat of stain and was considering going inside for a cup of coffee when he heard tires crunch on the driveway.

He walked around his pickup to see who it was. He rarely got visitors. He and Annie lived an hour from Calgary, on the outskirts of Way River, on five acres, most of which they leased to a local farmer. This year the farmer had planted canola and the house had sat in a sea of cheerful yellow all summer. Now the field looked forlorn with only the stubble left.

There were no close neighbors. Sometimes clients came but they always called ahead to get directions. And nobody ever dropped in to visit unless Annie was home. She was the social one.

The dark green, late-model Audi drove down the long driveway to the house, sunlight glancing off its tinted windows, then turned around at the wide spot before coming to a stop next to the house, where Annie usually parked, facing back toward the road. Luke wiped his hands on a rag and walked toward the back of the car, trying not to scowl. His jeans were a bit grubby and the front of his plaid shirt and his rolled-up sleeves were covered in stain but there was nothing he could do about it. He was a woodworker. He got dirty.

The driver's side door opened and a tall man stepped out, his back to Luke. The man wore jeans, too, but they were dark and new, clearly designer, and he wore gleaming cowboy boots to go with them. Luke rolled his eyes. When he focused on the red Western shirt and noticed its fringe and embroidery across the shoulders, he almost groaned.

"Nice place."

Luke kept control of his emotions but he couldn't stop the blood from leaving his face. That voice ... His gaze slowly moved from the ridiculous shirt to the back of the man's head. He finally turned around and grinned a familiar shit-eating grin.

"Bouca," said Luke softly.

Freddie Bouca laughed in delight, still standing in the open doorway of his Audi, one manicured hand on the car's roof. The fabric of his gaudy shirt stretched tight across his belly.

"I know, right?" he said. "How long's it been?"

"Fifteen years," said Luke. Fifteen years, four months and thirteen days. His hands tightened into fists. He slowly relaxed them.

The wind ruffled Luke's too-long, dark hair, sending shivers down his back. The wind rummaged through Bouca's black hair, too, making the trimmed and neat haircut look dishevelled. Except for the fact that Luke's hair showed no signs of gray or balding and Bouca now had a deep widow's peak and gray at his temples, they could have been brothers. They were both tall, with blue eyes.

Of course, Luke was much bigger than Bouca. Fifteen years of working with wood had kept him strong and in shape, where Bouca had developed a substantial gut. He looked a few years older than Luke's forty-five, but Luke knew he was actually closer to sixty.

"You're looking good, Luke," said Bouca, suddenly serious. "Marriage agrees with you." His lips twisted slightly and Luke braced himself.

"What do you want, Bouca?"

The smile came back. "Always direct," said Bouca. "I always admired that about you."

Luke waited. After a moment, the smile faded and Bouca said, "I need a favor."

Something cold and sharp moved through Luke's bowels.

"I don't do that kind of work anymore."

"So I hear!" said Bouca heartily. He nodded at the workshop behind Luke. "You're a carpenter now?"

"Cabinet maker," corrected Luke softly.

Bouca shrugged. "Okay. So you work out of a converted garage?" He studied the old garage behind the pickup.

Luke's shoulders tightened. Nothing had changed. Bouca still had to feel he was the smartest, richest, most ruthless. In the old days, if one of his competitors ended up with a fancier car than Bouca, somehow the competitor's car would go up in flames. At least Luke's house and converted garage posed no threat to Bouca, who lived in a mansion in Montreal's Westmount district. Or he used to.

Bouca looked at Luke. "Don't you ever worry about fire, with all that wood?"

Whatever he wanted, he must want it badly, to pull out veiled threats so early in the game.

"What do you want, Freddie?" asked Luke again. It felt strange, calling him by his first name. In the old days, he would never have done that.

Freddie Bouca dropped the smiles and the mock camaraderie. Suddenly his face looked gaunt and old. His chin dropped slightly and he looked directly at Luke.

"You owe me."

Luke took a deep breath to calm himself. Fifteen years, four months and thirteen days ago, he had walked away from the life—and from Bouca—when Bouca had ordered Luke to kill a man.

He didn't owe Freddie Bouca one goddamned thing. But Bouca apparently didn't see it that way.

"What do you want?" he asked for a third time. This time, there was a sharp edge to his voice.

"I need you to kill my lying, piece-of-shit wife."

For a second, Luke forgot to breathe. There was so much hate in Bouca's words that Luke felt them like sharp pinpricks to his chest. He cleared his throat.

"What did she do?" Not that it mattered.

Bouca's lips peeled back from his gritted teeth in a semblance of a smile.

"The bitch stole my kids and ran off to Calgary."

Fatigue rolled over Luke so fast he almost staggered. It was an old fatigue, one he thought he had left behind fifteen years ago. Was that how long Freddie Bouca had been keeping tabs on him? Had Luke always been at the end of Bouca's long tether?

"You need a lawyer, not me," Luke said.

Bouca took a deep breath, visibly trying to regain control.

"We're past that," he said. "Now we have to take care of things internally."

He wasn't *internal* to Bouca.

"I'm not in the business anymore," said Luke. "Even if I was, I don't do women or children. And I don't kill. You know that."

Bouca opened his mouth, but just then Luke's phone rang. Bouca closed his mouth and a wary expression came over his face. Luke pulled the phone out of his back pocket and looked at the screen. It was Annie's school.

He swiped the phone on.

"Hello?"

"Mr. Stonewell? This is Catherine at St. Joseph Elementary. Is Annie home sick today?"

For a moment, Luke couldn't speak. He looked up to find Bouca staring at him, his expression hard and unforgiving.

Luke found Annie's black Bronco parked on the shoulder of the range road she used as a shortcut to get to St. Joseph's. He pulled up behind it and jumped out of the pickup, leaving his door open. All four tires on the Bronco were intact so that wasn't why she had pulled over.

There were only a few farms along the road, and hardly any traffic. In winter, Annie took the long way around to humour him. That way, if her car broke down, at least there'd be other drivers around.

He scanned the inside of the Bronco and found nothing wrong. Her purse was gone, as was her lunch bag. As if the car had broken down and she had gotten a lift from someone.

He glanced around either side of the road, checked out the ditches and the empty field beyond it. No Annie.

He ran back to his pickup and swung inside. Bouca had given him two hours to get to an address in Calgary that was almost an hour away, kill Evangeline and text him the photo after it was done. Bouca would wait at the house until he heard from Luke. And in case Luke got any ideas, Bouca warned him, Annie would die unless Bouca got to her before the two hours were up.

Luke remembered how some of Bouca's enemies had died, all those years ago. He believed the man.

Not to worry, Bouca had assured him. Just get the job done and send the picture, and Bouca would set Annie free.

But Luke knew better.

He pulled the burner phone Bouca had given him out of his jeans pocket and stared at it. He knew nothing about cell phone technology. Did Bouca have a way of tracking him with the phone? Was it bugged?

He weighed it in his hand, trying to decide on a smart course of action but thoughts of his gentle Annie, trapped and frightened, kept intruding.

He would do her no good this way. He had to wipe the last fifteen years, four months and three days from his memory and revert to the hard man he'd once been.

He leaned across the front seat and reached into the glove box for the burner phone he always kept there. He pulled the charging cord out and plugged the phone in. He was rewarded with a green icon indicating the phone was charging.

He looked at the directory on the phone Bouca had given him. There was only one number, Bouca's. He entered that number into the directory of his own burner phone.

Then, with a flick of his wrist, he tossed Bouca's burner onto the pavement where it skidded into the wet ditch across the way.

He glanced around the deserted road once more before scrolling through the directory on his burner to find the number he wanted. He tapped it and waited for three excruciating seconds, praying the number was still active. Then it started ringing.

"Hello?" The woman who answered sounded like she was a three-pack-a-day smoker and scotch lover.

"Maxine," he said. Not Maxie. Not Max.

MYSTERY MAGAZINE

There was a long pause. Then a short bark of laughter.

"Fifteen years and you're still the only one who ever calls me by my given name, Luke."

Luke closed his eyes in relief. He didn't know if Maxine was still in the life—she had to be close to seventy now. Even if she had retired, she probably kept her finger on the pulse of whatever was happening in Montreal. She had treated him like a son, back then. Maybe she still had some residual affection for him.

"Maxine, I'm in trouble." The words came out more wobbly than he liked. He wasn't used to this anymore.

"What is it?" she said immediately, and he was glad he was sitting down, his relief was so great. Outside, a huge vee of geese flew by, heading south, honking.

"Freddie Bouca is here."

"Huh." She stayed silent for a bit and he could hear her take a drag from a cigarette. "You want to know what's going on then."

Luke nodded. "How many people does he have these days? Is he likely to have some with him?"

Maxine's answer was immediate.

"No. He's lost it all. He started going squirrely about a year ago, making crazy demands. He killed people for no good reason—some of his own people, Luke. So Joe Spanola took over and cut Freddie out. He had to give Freddie a solid beating to persuade him to accept the new reality. Only reason Freddie is still alive is some of the older guys argued against killing him."

Luke leaned his head back. Freddie Bouca was nuts. That explained a lot. He was also bluffing. Nobody was watching the clock to kill Annie if Bouca didn't show up before the two hours were up.

"What about his wife?" he asked.

"Evangeline?" Maxine snorted. "She packed her bags, took the girls and left. Nobody knows where she went. Or if they do, they're not sayin'."

"Freddie knows where they are," said Luke tiredly. "He wants me to kill her."

"Oh, baby," breathed Maxine. "You're not going to do it, are you?"

Luke stared at the Bronco parked in front of him.

"He took my wife, Maxine. Says he's going to kill her if I don't kill Evangeline."

There was a long silence at the other end. When Maxine spoke again, there was no emotion in her voice.

"He's going to kill her anyway. And he's going to try to kill you. He's sailed off the deep end, Luke. Your wife may already be dead."

He knew that, but it didn't help to hear it spoken out loud.

"Thanks, Maxine. I needed to know the lay of the land." Bouca was on his own, unsanctioned. "Why doesn't he kill Evangeline himself?"

Maxine thought for a moment. "He wants his kids. He knows that the cops will look at him for the murder. He wants distance."

And he didn't trust any of his former associates. It was just Luke's bad luck that he lived close to Calgary.

"You're not going to kill her, are you?" asked Maxine sharply.

"I don't do women or kids," said Luke. "And I don't kill. You know that."

Bouca had shown up at the house about an hour after Annie left. And Luke had found her Bronco five minutes from home. That meant that Bouca had stashed her maybe twenty-five minutes away, factoring in the time to tie her up and lock her in.

Or kill her and hide her.

Don't go there, he told himself. Bouca would hang on to Annie as a hostage, to make sure Luke did as he was told.

That's what a sane man would do.

He thought through all the places Bouca could have left Annie. There were too many—from barns to cow shelters to coulees …

He didn't have time to search them all before Bouca's deadline. How would he ever find her in time?

He couldn't. Not unless he forced Bouca to tell him.

He glanced at his watch. He'd used up half an hour of Bouca's allotted two hours.

"Hello?"

Luke drove with one hand and pressed the phone against his ear with the other. "Is this Evangeline?"

There was a pause, then the woman's voice came back. "Yes. Who is this?"

Now it was Luke's turn to pause. How to say this?

Bluntly, he decided.

"Evangeline, take your kids and go to the police. Right now. Freddie has found you and he wants to kill you."

He hung up and dialed 9-1-1.

"9-1-1," came a man's voice. "What is your emergency?"

"Listen carefully," said Luke. "A man called Freddie Bouca is in Calgary. He plans to murder his estranged wife and kidnap his children. The wife's name is Evangeline and this is her address." He read off the address from the scrap of paper Bouca had given him. "I've already warned her but her kids may be in school. Send someone to her place now."

"Sir—"

Luke hung up, hoping it was enough. He'd lied about Bouca's whereabouts—no point leading the police to his own back yard. He turned off his burner phone and tossed it out the window. He'd already written down Maxine's and Bouca's phone numbers on the back of Bouca's scrap of paper.

Even harvested, the canola field surrounding Luke and Annie's house stank like an old gym bag left in a locker over the summer. Luke pressed on, watching where he put his feet among the dry stubble. He had left the pickup on the access road the farmer used and was sneaking up to the house from the back. There were sliding glass doors on the back that led to a patio, but the garage blocked him from view. Besides, at this time of day, the sun would glare at anyone looking out the windows on that side of the house.

Still, he felt exposed in the empty field. A walking target.

He had to hope that Bouca would be sitting at the kitchen counter, or in the living room, whose picture window faced the driveway and the road.

He crouched as he moved forward. A small, hard-packed dirt buffer separated the field from the back lawn. Directly in front of him was the back of the vinyl-clad garage. He would have to go around it to see the driveway.

He emerged from the field at a run and flattened himself against the back of the garage. The sun beat down on him but the wind was cold. He was just in his plaid woolen shirt and undershirt, but the activity kept him warm.

He eased his head past the corner of the garage and studied the back of the house. No one outside. No Freddie Bouca staring back at him from the patio doors or the windows. He couldn't see the Audi from this angle.

With a deep breath, he stepped away from the garage and ran toward the corner of the house, only to stumble to a halt at the sound of gravel crunching under wheels. He peered around the corner.

The Audi was driving away.

Luke watched just long enough to see which direction it would turn, then he went tearing back through the canola field.

Had Freddie seen him? Was that why he left?

By the time he reached the access road and his pickup, he was out of breath but there was no time to waste. He hauled himself into the driver's seat, started the engine and tore down the access road. He didn't even come to a stop once he reached the road but fishtailed onto it, heading in the same direction Bouca had taken.

He drove fast, trying to catch up to the Audi, which had disappeared in the distance. As he approached each side road or access road, he slowed down to peer into the distance, trying to see a gleam of green.

Where was Bouca going? To catch the highway toward Calgary? To kill Annie? Or was she already dead and lying in a coulee?

The fear rose up so quickly in his chest that he almost choked.

He had to get a grip. The guy he used to be wouldn't get sidetracked by emotion. He had to be that guy.

But he wasn't that guy anymore. He was Annie's husband. A woodworker. A peaceful man. And Annie was a gentle soul who had no experience with the life.

He caught a flash of green out of the corner of his eye and then it was gone. There. An old barn, half fallen in. The big wooden doors were ajar. As he watched, they closed.

That was where the son of a bitch had taken Annie.

Luke wished he hadn't tossed Bouca's burner phone. He didn't know what help it could have been but tossing it felt like a strategic miscalculation.

Strategy had never been his strong suit. He'd always gone wherever the wind pushed him, which was how he'd ended up as one of Freddie Bouca's enforcers at seventeen. He'd liked the pay, the women, the booze. And all he'd had to do was "tune up" people who owed Bouca some money. Or drugs.

At seventeen, he'd already been six foot and a hundred and eighty pounds. He had big fists and an affinity for fighting.

After a while, he started studying for his GED. It took a couple of years but he finally got his high school diploma. He began reading about woodworking and tried his hand at small projects in his apartment in the St-Henri district. He loved it. He dreamed of having his own workshop one day.

By the time he was twenty-five, he'd gained an inch and twenty pounds, all muscle. He'd also gained perspective. He realized he didn't like Freddie Bouca or the people Bouca associated with. Himself included.

He was thirty when he met Annie. She was twenty-six, a school teacher, a five-foot-three bundle of curves, attitude and humour. She had just moved to Montreal from Vancouver. He fell in love with her the first time he heard her laugh. And to his ever-lasting wonder, she fell in love with him too.

He never told her what he did for a living. He'd often thought of confessing—he was pretty sure her heart was large enough to forgive him—but he never plucked up the nerve.

The day Bouca asked Luke to murder a man, he and Annie each packed a suitcase and left Montreal. In Toronto, Luke sold his car and bought a sedan. They headed for Vancouver to visit Annie's family before moving to Alberta where Annie had secured a job teaching in Way River.

He mailed Maxine a card before he left Montreal telling her he was leaving and apologizing for not saying goodbye. He always liked the older woman and didn't want her wondering if he was alive or dead.

In Way River, he reinvented himself. He had enough money stashed away to almost buy their little house outright. He bought tools and books and wood, and for the first Christmas fair, he had bookshelves, side tables and burl bowls. And business cards.

Today, he was making furniture, designing staircases, chairs, rocking chairs ... anything made out of wood. And Annie had been offered the position of vice-principal, though she wasn't sure she wanted to give up teaching.

No children, but maybe that was just as well. He didn't want any child inheriting his violent streak. Annie would have liked children, but theirs was a good life.

Until Freddie Bouca showed up.

Luke didn't bother looking for an access road. He crossed the shallow ditch, splashing water up the sides of his truck, then crossed the shorn field toward the barn. He was making too much noise but it couldn't be helped. Every instinct in him screamed at him to hurry.

When he reached the dilapidated barn, he stepped on the gas and plowed right through the doors, smashing them into splinters that flew over his windshield and deeper into the barn. He immediately slammed on the brakes, in case the Audi was just inside, and squinted at the gloomy interior.

He saw the Audi first, only ten feet from his bumper. Then he threw himself out of the pickup before he even registered the sight of Freddie Bouca standing in front of the open trunk of his Audi, gun in hand.

A gun. That had never been Freddie's way and Luke hadn't expected it. Now despair washed over him as Bouca shot at him, shattering the driver's side window and showering Luke with glass. If Bouca killed him, there'd be no hope for Annie.

Before Luke could even think about a next step, Freddie grunted and something metallic clattered onto the barn's concrete floor. Luke risked a glance around the open door of his truck.

Bouca was holding his arm, a look of shock on his face. The gun lay on the floor a few feet away. A movement caught Luke's eye and he spotted Annie climbing out of the trunk of the Audi, a lug wrench in hand.

The look of rage on her face made him catch his breath. Her hair was dishevelled and bloody, and her red jacket was torn at the shoulder. A swelling on the right side of her face distorted her features and promised to turn purple soon. That son of a bitch had hit her.

With fury in her eyes, she looked like the goddess of war.

Luke was around the pickup's door and stalking toward the injured man when Freddie saw him and scrambled for the gun. He'd barely reached it when the lug wrench landed on the back of his head with all the force an enraged Annie could put into it. Freddie jerked at the blow, his scalp torn open, bloody bone showing through.

He dropped like a felled tree and blood gushed out, immediately surrounding Bouca's head in a pool of scarlet.

By then Luke was close enough to wrap a big hand around Annie's hand and lower her arm. When she looked at him, he didn't recognize the fury standing in front of him.

"Annie," he said firmly.

She turned away and tried to free her arm, clearly intent on hitting Bouca again.

"Annie!" Her name came out sharp and it seemed to work. She looked at Luke—really looked at him—and the fury retreated.

"Luke?" she said, and then she started trembling. The lug wrench dropped from her hand with a clatter and she gazed at Freddie Bouca.

"Did I kill him?" she asked softly.

Luke squeezed her arm and released her to go check on Bouca. The man's skull was split open, with gray matter oozing out. Luke placed a finger on his neck to check for a pulse but he knew there wouldn't be one. Bouca's eyes were open.

"He's dead," he said.

"He was going to kill you," said Annie. "He was going to kill *me*!" Her voice was full of wonder. "I'd never seen him before. He had pulled over on the side of the road and was waving me to a stop. I thought he was in trouble. When I got out of the Bronco, he hit me." She kept staring at Bouca, so Luke turned her away. "He knocked me out. I woke up when he opened the trunk. He had his gun out and wanted me to get out."

She waved at the Audi and Luke took his first look at the barn. Half the roof was caving in at the back end, and one wall had partially fallen into stalls.

"Come on," he said, wrapping an arm around her shoulders. "Let's get out of here."

"Are we going to call the police?" she asked, following him obediently.

"Yes," said Luke. There was no point trying to hide this. Annie was covered with blood. The trunk would have traces of her. The lug wrench would have her fingerprints. And he was pretty sure the police had ways of tracking the burner phones he had tossed. And there were bullet holes in his truck. It was all going to come back to him.

But he had done nothing but try to find his wife. And Annie had done nothing but defend herself and protect him.

But that wasn't the whole of it, was it? This was all his fault. His past had followed him to Way River and turned Annie into a killer.

He lifted her into the passenger seat of the pickup and stood looking at her.

"But first, I need to tell you something."

She blinked at him, her right eye bloodshot and swelling shut.

"Is it about what you used to do before you met me?" Despite the swelling and the trembling, she was already starting to regain her composure. Already returning to herself.

A self Luke realized he had never really known. He would never have thought his sweet wife could kill someone. For any reason.

He took a deep breath and kept his hands to himself. He really wanted to hold hers but she might never want to touch him again after he finished telling her.

"Yes," he said.

Annie pulled at his arm and took his hand in hers.

"I know, sweetheart. I think I've always known." She took a deep breath. "Not the details, of course. I don't think we need to discuss it. Who you were doesn't matter. Who you are is who I love." Annie nodded to the still figure on the floor. "Who is that man?"

"That was my old boss," he said. "He took you to force me to kill his ex-wife."

Annie's head jerked back even as her hand tightened on his.

"You didn't, did you?"

Luke smiled crookedly and looked away. A day ago, he would never have thought she could ask him such a question.

"No," he said softly. "I don't do women or children. And I don't kill."

She looked at him, a complex mix of compassion and grief in her eyes. "But I do."

TAM HINKLE'S LAST SUNDOWN

Richard Prosch

The storyteller's life isn't as flush as it used to be, and I guess I was a thistlehead for not seein' it sooner. The pulp magazines went to Boot Hill years ago and the digests are gone to dust. Cold war spies and moon rockets are all the rage, and the name Archie Echols doesn't pull any more weight with the paperback mills. An old key-puncher like me spinnin' yarns about cowboys and cattle drives can't hardly make beans and board in the space age. Nothing I can do but lean on an inheritance from Agatha, my wife of forty years—may she rest in peace.

I can't say I've penned any real prose in quite a spell.

More than once, I've considered chucking the old Smith Corona off under a Death Valley cactus and retiring to Vegas. Likely that's where I'd be right now if an ad in back of one of the film magazines hadn't put a bug in my head—and let me tell you, that varmint went to work churning up a deep well of memories, dark and brackish.

That morning, my breakfast table was a basement bar looking out a pair of glass doors at our hacienda patio and the arid California landscape. Before she passed, Agatha had the place decorated real nice in avocado green and yellow ochre and my velvet matador painting on the north wall nailed the Western mood.

I sipped at my vodka-seasoned orange juice, stared through wiggles of shimmering heat at the abandoned lot across the way, and pretended it was old Mexico and I was a rootin' tootin' six-shooter.

Then I looked at the typewriter, at the blank piece of paper all snug in its place, waiting for me.

To kill some more time, I flipped through a movie mag on the bar until this advert I mentioned grabbed me by the short hairs.

Between the periodical's heavy print for hernia belts and skin softeners, the publisher pitched woo to the silent film starlets of old with three lusty lines and the promise of a gravy train. "Movie flappers of the 1920s," it read, "did you drive grand dad mad in his favorite flickers? Let your voice finally be heard. Big money paid for your real life story!"

I wasn't surprised at the nostalgic appeal. Some of the two-reelers have seen some interest on the college campus lately, and a full-fledged Tom Mix revival is happening over at the Lux Theater on Paradise street.

While us oldsters were marveling at color TV, the kids were flocking back to Broncho Billy and William S. Hart.

You'd think it would translate into the Western book market, but no.

I was broke as a ten-key piano.

When I saw those three words:

Big.

Money.

Paid.

I slapped the mag shut, determined to get me some.

Big money paid for your real-life story.

Archie Echols had a story alright, but it wasn't all mine. Mixed up in the plot was a gal pal from the silent photoplay days—a bombshell they branded Tam Hinkle in the press, but her real name was Stella Toups.

I got on good with Tam in those days before I knew Agatha.

Here's how it was. Back in the '20s, I got high rates for my stuff, knocking out thousands of words a day for the pulps. Meanwhile, Tam lounged under the electric lights and made a fortune getting her moving picture made. At night we drained our paychecks together, and stayed chums even after I got married and she got divorced.

Me and Tam, we both had more dough than common sense, and our hormones ran as fast as the horses down at the track.

Then one day just before the stocks crashed, she asked to borrow my rocking chair.

A weird request—completely out of the blue—and not at all the kind of bourgeois thing you'd expect from a glamour queen who spent every waking moment surrounded by money men, imported cheese, and the finest in bootleg rum.

Tam had seen the Victorian-era mahogany rocker in my den, but darned if I could remember her ever sitting in it.

Whenever she came by the den we spent most of our time on the couch.

The chair was handmade by my dad, Archie Sr., with a hole in the seat covered with button upholstered leather. It was all I had left of the old man, so when she asked if she could borrow it, I said, "Not for free!" and we cobbled together a swap.

Tam got the chair and I got, well ... let's say something of value from her.

I figured she wanted the chair for a movie prop.

Boy-oh-boy, I was as green as they came in those days despite my high-falootin' status with the wordslingers back East. There's only one reason a young gal wants a rocking chair from the hoi poloi, and when she drew me a picture, I hit the damn-blasted roof.

Like I'd never heard of the birds and the bees.

We went at it for more than an hour, me hurling insults and peppery names, her tossing a coffee cup and an ashtray. It ended when I slammed her penthouse apartment door in her face.

A violent parting of the ways to be sure, and I think both of us vowed revenge.

Neither of us ever got it.

The night we argued was the last I saw Tam Hinkle in the flesh. So to speak.

So that morning I came across the magazine ad, I crunched some ice from my juice glass and gazed out across the desert feeling a wave of emotion I hadn't felt in decades.

The little hussy never did bring back my chair.

And it made me mad.

With the magazine ad still working on me, I walked across my orange shag carpet on bare feet, twisted the combination on my wall safe, and opened the door.

The old Colt Walker .44 pistol was right where I knew it would be, nickel plated and gleaming in the early morning sunshine. I picked up the gun, carried it to the center of my basement and pulled back the hammer.

"They want a story, they're going to get it," I told myself.

Thinking about that chair had me seein' red.

The sun broke over the horizon, and I spun the Colt's cylinder in the light of a brand new day.

It was gonna be a reckoning day for Tam Hinkle.

Above the low slung abodes at Hobbs Court with their long straight lines and flat panes of glass and cement, a chunky stucco beast crouched as if to pounce. The monster mansion was ablaze with turquoise window panes and brick red ceramic shingles. I hadn't seen the Spanish Colonial revival house of Tam Hinkle and her dead husband, Bud, since 1956. That was the same year as my gallbladder operation, Hobbs Court being on the way to Mt. Sinai hospital.

That sunny afternoon after I'd seen the movie magazine ad, I let the brakes on my old '56 Buick Roadmaster drag me to a stop behind a cactus thirty feet from the house—far enough away, I hoped, not to be seen by the neighbors. I climbed out from behind the wheel and made five full strides in my gator-skin boots toward the long, curving driveway before thumping my noggin and spinning on a heel.

Sometimes I'm so boneheaded they oughta bleach my horns and hang me for a saloon decoration. Here I charted my way through the simmering desert sand to the other side of town only to forget what I came for.

Making sure the neighborhood busy bodies were keeping a nose to themselves, I slipped into the convertible's passenger seat and cracked the cubby to retrieve the old Colt Walker.

I liked the heft of the gun in my hand. The weight, the cold, smooth finish, the sense of history. Everything about the piece brought back memories of using the gun in countless stories I penned over two generations.

In "Gunshot Trail," my drover used the Colt to escape a hangman's noose with a barrage of lead. In "Fortune's Buzzard," the Colt perforates a villain's black Stetson hat. "Ride for the Brand" saw the debut of Two-Colt Kim, the closest thing I ever got to a recurring hero.

I brought the gun close to my chest, rubbing it like a magic talisman. That's exactly what it was in "Six-Shot Mojo," a good-luck charm for the cowman therein.

But only after he fired it off.

Funny thing. As I stood outside Tam Hinkle's mansion caressing the gun—I realized I'd never fired the Colt in real life.

The irony was still on my mind when I marched up to Tam's big front door and pressed the buzzer.

Seein' myself standin' there that way, reflected in the glass of her storm door with my high-water butternut britches, plaid jacket, and wide apricot colored tie, I pert-near turned tail and skedaddled away. My dark hair had gone gray. My jowls hung like a bulldog. The big innertube around my waistline sagged. Old Tam wouldn't know me from Adam, and I thought it was important she know me right away.

She certainly wasn't expecting me.

But I wanted the memories to flood in on first glance. I wanted her to remember how we broke up and about the chair.

I kept the gun hid behind my back.

Of course it would be a servant answered the door. "Yes?" said the old broomstick.

"Tam Hinkle?" I inquired.

The lady cocked her head like I spoke in Portuguese. "May I ask who's calling?" she said.

"Tell her it's ... tell her it's an old friend. A writer she once knew."

"I'm afraid I—"

"Just tell her," I said, finding comfort then in the old maid's ragged appearance. Her long sleeves were frayed at the cuffs, her waistbelt partially undone. The skirt clinging to her toothpick legs was as dark as her blouse, but a stitch of red embroidery at the hem had strings trailing like cobwebs.

"Won't you come in?" she said.

I stepped into an atmosphere of potpourri dust and furniture wax, the foyer filled with a baby grand Steinway, every nook and cranny around it overflowing with dry, limping flowers. The ceiling was twenty feet high, and a white carpeted stairway spiraled up behind the piano.

Hanging on the wall, eight feet tall was a black and white portrait of Tam Hinkle in her prime, her face pancake white, her ebony lips in a coquettish smirk, her dark lined eyes peering into my soul. She was beautiful and terrible, accusing and absolutely innocent.

How I once loved her.

"Lovely, wasn't she?" said the old lady, lifting her chin, pulling out one of her long gray curls and tucking it up close to her graceful jawline. The skin was pale parchment, the eyes like smoldering coal.

How could I not have recognized her?

"She was indeed," I said.

"And now? Is she still?"

Tam turned to me with her whimsical smile. "It's been a long time, Arch."

All I could do was nod, my hands sweaty on the gun behind my back, the lump in my throat like a fresh horse apple, making me wanna retch.

I followed her eyes to a spot beside the piano.

The rocking chair waited between two potted ferns, its rosewood luster shining like new, the brass upholstery tacks gleaming against the unmarred leather seat. The years had fallen away. Fully restored, it was better than when I'd loaned it to her all those decades ago.

Tam answered my questioning look.

"I had it redone for you a few years ago. There's a furniture place I know in the valley. I always meant to have it delivered, but I ..." she let the words drift in the air between us, a whisper, "I don't know."

"You wanted to deliver it in person?" I asked.

After a while she said, "Maybe you're right."

On top of the piano, a line of glass-front photo frames made an orderly procession of young folks. Two girls, three boys. I nodded my head toward the pictures. "Your children?"

"The only real success I ever had," said Tam. "All of them spent time in your rocker, Archie. One after another, down through the years." Her face beamed with quiet pride. "My first and second grandchild too. Your old chair is sort of an institution around here."

"Speaking of institutions," I said.

"Are you still writing, Arch?"

"I came over to ..."

Tam shook her head. "You wrote the damnedest things."

The old gal hadn't changed so much after all, I thought. Never letting me finish a sentence, starting out at a slow boil, but hell for leather once she got primed. I knew from experience I needed to cut to the chase or forever hold my peace.

"You remember what you traded me for the chair?" I said.

Her eyes sparkled. "I do."

I brought the gun around from behind my back, and she ran toward me, embracing it with both hands.

"The Silver Colt," she cried, and her voice cracked like a lake of ice in the January thaw. "You kept it all these years."

"Guess it sorta got to be a ... what was the word you used? An institution with me, just like the chair did for you."

She hugged the gun to her bosom, then traced the initials hammered into the ivory grip. "T.M," she said. "I got this from Mr. Mix on my twenty-first birthday."

"I like to think his spirit stayed close," I said.

"You continued with Western stories?"

I told her I did.

"And you're doing alright? You're still writing?"

I admitted I'd slacked off some.

Tam held the Colt in both hands, pointing it up to the cathedral ceiling, twirling like a ballerina. Or like an angel expecting to take flight.

I thanked heaven the damn thing wasn't loaded.

"There's tea in the other room. If you've got a few minutes?"

I looked up at the portrait. "For the queen of the silver screen, I've got the rest of the day."

She reached for my hand, and I accepted it.

"Archie, the woman in the portrait rode off into the sunset decades ago."

"Did she?"

"Tam Hinkle's last sundown was the day you said goodbye," she said. "Call me Stella."

"Stella," I said, and she led me down the hallway into the foyer where a silver tea set waited.

We had a lot of stories to tell.

And to hell with the movie magazine.

SOLD AT AUCTION

Nicolas Calcagno

The sandstone cliff face cracks, and chips rain down off the rim through light and brutal heat into the canyon. They crash onto the paved parking lot of a café—the only sign of humanity—for hundreds of miles of rocky mountain desert. A group of oversized ravens briefly scatter from the commotion before regrouping. A cloud of dust appears on the horizon a visually indeterminate distance away. Minutes pass as the dust stirs up through the waving lines of heat, getting closer, but the ravens are undisturbed. More time passes, and finally, the birds move again, hopping a few feet away, as a little electric blue Mini Cooper pulls in front of the Outlaw Café.

Penny steps out, putting on his sunglasses and furrowing his eyes at the birds.

"It's too bright, is what it is," he says to the ravens, it seems. They regard him in reply.

Walking past and into the café, he cringes, surprised, from the din of the restaurant. He takes his sunglasses off.

Loud, over some unseen speaker system, plays the music of Glen Campbell, while a pretty, leathered waitress of middle age attends to a handful of chatty tables with her shaky hands.

"Seat yourself, gun," the waitress says, angling her head to one booth in particular. The café is styled, it must be said, by a particular hand losing its grip on sanity in a particular way. Guns, of every kind, from every era, from the lever-action Winchesters that won the American West to the automated rifles of suburban boat salesmen, to oversized novelty sheriff's pistols, hang on the walls. They hang next to iron animal yokes, above well-cared-for desert fronds, by inspirational posters extolling self-sufficiency and a short fuse for tyranny. Everywhere, always, guns, guns, guns.

Penny sidles into a booth with a poster of American Hero John Wayne hanging on the wall just above the table. It has a little quote by American President Ronald Reagan: "There was never a man like him, and he will be missed."

"What can I get you, gun," the waitress asks.

"Sorry?," Penny replies.

"What can I get you, gun?"

"Oh, ah, weird. OK." He glances at the menu. The first option is two home-made biscuits covered in sausage gravy. A diner classic. It's called "The Gun Fight."

"I guess I'll have a The Gun Fight. Is that alright?" Penny asks.

"Fine by me. Give me ten minutes."

Seven minutes later, she returns with a glistening plate of Southern comfort. The smell of the food more than makes up for the décor, he thinks. The waitress stands by the table for the quick moment it takes Penny to leave the plate empty.

"Didn't like it at all, did you?"

Before he has time to answer, she fires another question at him.

"You going out towards Canyonlands, gun? Can't think of another reason anyone like you would be out this way," she says.

"Yup. Driving out there for a few days for some qua-li-ty time. The great outdoors and all that, right."

She gives him a wide and lopsided grin.

"Oh, yea. *All* that. Well, if you're going that way, why don't you take the road down by the river? That highway out there's all bookcase cliffs, nothing but cliffs, and more of 'em. But it splits off and goes down to Scola. Us locals we call it the Scola exit, but I guess we can't anymore. Not with *everything* going on in this country. Here, let me show you," and the waitress sits down next to Penny without so much as a respectful look at him.

She pulls her phone up and opens some alternative to Google Maps he's never seen before. Her location settings, which are off, mean she has to type in the address for the Outlaw Café in the Start box. She notices him notice and announces: "Can't ever be too careful with these companies. You know these apps all track you nowadays."

A murmur of agreement comes from some nearby patrons, who absorbed her last comment seemingly through osmosis.

"You never know, I guess," Penny mumbles in reply.

"Just trust me, gun. I do know, and you can't. So, here you go: You take that highway another ten miles, when it splits take the exit on the left—looks like it's still called the Scola exit, what do you know—"

"Not for long, I bet though!" a patron yells out.

"Not for long. Ain't that true. You take the Scola exit, keep on that way by the river, down through the canyon and you'll pop up right by the start of Canyonlands. Well worth it by my book. Sound good?" The waitress stands up from the booth, finally looking him in the eyes, expectantly.

"Yea, sounds nice," Penny replies, catching his breath from eating so quickly.

"Hey, you think you can fill up this water skein while I run to the bathroom? Can't have enough water out there."

"Better than you filling it up while you're in the bathroom, I say, gun. Sure thing," and the waitress whisks away into the kitchen.

Penny walks into the restroom, where an old, cryptic poster of a gun in high heels stands above the toilet. A small, framed sign alongside it implores the viewer to Scratch 'n' Sniff and thanks John Jenkins for kindly donating the artwork. Penny chooses to ignore the sign.

He pays at the register and thanks the waitress.

"No problem, gun. And remember, sometimes, the blood of patriots must be spilled to escape the binds of tyranny."

"I was about to say that. Thanks."

The heat of the day outside envelops him like a padded hand. A few more ravens have joined the original crowd, and the jury stands, pecking his rear left tire with sporadic, staccato strikes.

"Hey! Fuckin'... stop that. Shoo!" he yells, running over, waving his arms over his head the way he imagines would scare a collection of birds.

The birds, completely unafraid, take a few little hops away from the car and stop, silently judging him.

"Ok, well, like, thanks for nothing, assholes. Bye, I guess."

Distant cliffs stand still as the parallax of open spaces dwarfs the triple-digit speed of the car. Rocky desert turns to red silts and, soon, the road runs next to the muddy green of the shallow Colorado River—the unassuming liquid buzzsaw that carved this canyon out of stone over millions of years.

Every so often, a brief glance up at the roadside canyon wall reveals another jury of ravens, watching silently, as Penny, his car, and his music—an up-tempo, high-frequency, European drum and bass song with lyrics pitched up somewhere behind the synths and beats—disturb the silence of their rock courtroom.

Tires grasping the road as the weight of the little vehicle shifts out towards the turn, Penny vibes, riding down the highway. Far up ahead, more ravens gather on the river embankment around some roadkill, which seems to crawl towards the street. He slows down and sees they surround a surprisingly large bipedal creature. Slowing nearly to a stop, he realizes the roadkill isn't an animal at all, and, given the first realization, thankfully, is also not dead. Now, nearly a foot into the road, a bloodied man, hair mottled with scabs and desert silt, body covered in grime, inches forward slowly, each movement a stubborn step against the journey to Hell.

Penny runs shouting from the car.

"Hey! Shit, man. OK? Are you OK?"

Something about this injured man registers with Penny. The fellow is in no shape to respond.

"Oh, fuck, fuck. No, not supplements. No echinacea, hm, acupuncture won't help either. Well, maybe it could, if I use the really good stuff."

He runs to the trunk, where he'd stashed the blanket he'd stolen off the airplane on the way out here, and tosses it across the backseat. Lifting the guy into the rear of the car and stretching him out sideways, he realizes the guy is groaning words at him.

"No ... no os..tal."

"I can't understand you, I'm sorry man. I just don't know what you're saying."

"No osital," the fellow groans again.

Penny pours some water into the man's cracked, dirty throat.

He hacks and hacks, turning so red, Penny thinks he's dying, which he might be, although presumably not from asphyxiation, until finally he scratches out a full sentence.

"Jesus. Are you trying to drown me? No fucking hospital," and the fellow falls back, asleep.

When he comes to, Penny has moved him from the car into a bedroom—decorated wall-to-wall with all sorts of stone and crystal totems. The man sits up, nearly perforating his forehead on the inside half of an amethyst geode hanging unsafely over the bed.

"I didn't take you the hospital like you asked. But I should've, man. What if you'd fucking died?" Penny asks him.

"Yes, well. I didn't. And thank you kindly for not doing that. Thank you for taking care of me. When is it?"

"Like, what year?"

The man cuts Penny off.

"What are you saying? No. What day is it? I haven't known what day it is since I got lost."

"It's, uh, Wednesday the 25th. That cool with you?" Penny asks.

The man furrows his brow. He looks older than his age, Penny thinks, maybe 40 or so, with a few thick creases stuck in the center of his forehead.

"Yes, it is quite alright. Just fine, really."

He pats his pockets, finding them empty. On the nightstand just off to the side, he spots his wallet, spread open and face down.

"Well, what is your name? I feel at a disadvantage given," the man gestures towards the wallet with some tightness in his voice, "that."

"Penny," adding at the man's stare of clear disbelief: "it's just a nickname, it's not a boy named Sue thing," flexing his bicep in sort-of mock Mr. Olympia pose.

"Great. Karl Perdue, as I'm sure you know. Nice to meet you."

"Still. Better to hear it from the horse's mouth, I always say. How's the investment business treating you, Karl?"

Karl straightens up a little, producing a small cough as he does.

"How do you—"

"Eh, Googled you while you were out there. You were asleep the better part of two days. I needed *something* fun to do. I felt myself slipping into some very negative thought patterns alone, so I thought I'd check you out a bit."

A few moments pass before Karl shrugs a "what-can-you-do" shrug with his hands and shoulders, and slowly brings his feet off to the side of the bed.

"It's going well. I have a real estate meeting later today, actually. So, if it doesn't bother you, and if in your expert medical opinion, I am safe for release from the clinic, I'll take my absence, friend," Karl says, in a not quite friendly tone.

"So, that's it, man? No real thank you? Nothing?"

Standing up and walking as hurriedly as a still-injured man can, Karl says over his shoulder: "Fair enough. If you're ever in Moab, come by the Legendary Silver Dollar Saloon. I'll be giving out free drinks by the time you walk in the door," and he leaves in the late-afternoon lull.

"But, we're already in Moab. So much for Western hospitality. Is that something people say?" Penny asks the now-empty room.

Like a bored man with nothing to do, which, coincidentally, is exactly what Penny is in this moment, he looks around the rented Airbnb whose vibes had so resonated with him back home in the city. They still do, if a little less, in the wake of Karl's emotional vortex.

The décor runs close to spiritual mid-century modern, with the aforementioned crystals and now-mentioned dreamcatchers hanging nailed above a smart collection of shining teak furniture. A newspaper and a number 2 pencil sit on the middle leaf of a dinner table. Penny walks to the table successfully, only stumbling once when he catches his foot on a fold in the psychedelic tapestry that functions as the apartment's rug.

Moab's Lightning Spiders had beaten Muscogee's Dirty Mares resoundingly, 42 to 7, with a strong showing by their defense, forcing six fumbles, two of which they recovered and returned for touchdowns. The editorial board celebrated a crowdfunding campaign to raise money for one of its ex-delivery men who'd they'd laid off the year before, after being purchased by Stonefield Investments—all information included in the editorial. Penny skims the third story in the paper, some marquee investigation into financial corruption in the Moab real estate market, who cares, before flipping to the classifieds.

One missing persons report (too obvious, they ran away), a notice for a property tax sale in town, a handful of power tools for sale, one horse for sale, and then one more missing person—this one a little more interesting. "Church pastor missing. You don't know this denomination. Please help. Blessed be the Wave. 435-093-0585."

Penny pulls his cellphone from his pocket and sets it on the table. He scoops up the faded off-white house phone, and punches in the numbers.

"Jenkins Horse and Mule Barn, hay or grain?" a gruff man answers.

"Blessed be the Wave?" Penny offers.

"Oh, fuckin—not you goddamn assholes again."

Using his keen powers of observation, Penny realizes this man is not with the Blessed be the Wave folks.

"No, no, my bad, man. Not really a nice way to answer the phone, but I'm not with those guys. I'm a detective. Is this 435-093-0585?"

"Some detective you must be. This is 435-093-0644," the gruff man answers before sighing, exhausted, and hanging up the phone.

Wow. Didn't even really come close to the right number.

"I need to up my Hazelnut extract," thinks Penny.

He dials again. This time, the line connects but no one speaks. A breath draws softly in and out on the other end and he feels his throat tighten just a little.

"Blessed be the Wave?" Penny whispers.

For a moment, nothing, not even the breath, then a few small good-natured giggles exhaled through the nose.

A woman speaks in a friendly tone: "You know that's not the name, right? It's ... like a blessing for after sermons. We're generally known as The Church of the Yellow Wave, or Wavies, or ..." she pauses, before doing her best imitation of a man with a deep voice, "those goddamn assholes."

"Hey! I just talked to someone who called you ... well, that."

"You talked with Jenkins Horse and Mule Barn? Honestly, Jenkins is an alright guy. He's just tired. It's not the best time for a hay and grain distributor out here."

He hears a vacancy settle into her voice, like part of her disappeared into an inner world he'd never know.

"He's 88 years old. He's seen this place go from an outlaw hideout, where explorers prospected for fossils in the canyons by day and drank until gunshots rang out at night, to a … Well, now, whatever it is now …" she pauses and then continues "it's just an amusement park. Just a place to buy rocks and call yourself a nature-lover."

Her voice picks up again.

"That's why you're calling, right? About my ad?"

Penny wants to help her. He wanted to help the ad-writer, but now he wants to help *her*.

Summoning as much professionalism as possible, Penny replies.

"Yes, ma'am. I saw your request in the classified section of the newspaper and was shaken by a congregation's loss of their leader. It just doesn't seem right. My name's Penny, and I'm a detective. How can I help?" He tries his best not to exhale audibly, tired out from the rare professionalism and all.

"Wow, shaken, huh? Some speech. Well, thank you, Penny. I'm Angie." A quick inhale. "I guess I should say, I'm not a Wavie anymore. I joined the church a few years ago and stayed with them until just a few weeks ago. Nothing happened, before you ask," she says nervously, "I just didn't want to go anymore. Part of me still believes in the Yellow Wave, you know, the healing rays, the Holy Stone, transcendence through pain, all that. Part of me doesn't, anymore, is all."

She sounds sad as she says this. Maybe her first time telling anyone outside the church about her changed faith, making her thoughts real through words. Maybe she'd never even said it quite like that, never even thought it quite like that, feeling a piece of her chest unlock as this truth opens up some space in her heavy heart.

"Hey, are you listening to me?" Angie asks.

Shit. He is not.

"Yes, of course I am. I am a detective, and I'm listening, like a detective would." Penny starts waving the tip of the pencil randomly across the newspaper, hoping to mimic the sounds of an attentive notetaker.

"Really? Because it was dead silent, and then right when I asked that, you started scribbling wildly."

Shit. That is what happened.

"Ok, let's not focus too much on who might be or maybe wasn't listening, and let's talk about the case."

"Yea, ok, so, literally like I was saying, last week our pastor, *the* pastor, I should say, Jon Stillman, went hiking with a friend out in Arches. It was hot. Like, 108 degrees hot. Hot enough to fry an egg, as they say. Nobody's seen either one of them since. They've both done this a thousand times, just not when it's this hot. I told him. It was too hot. I *told him, goddamit.*"

She takes a deep breath and exhales.

"I'm afraid they went too far and ran out of water or got delirious and walked the wrong way. I tried talking to the Park Service, and they sent out a search team, but didn't find anything. I know it doesn't look good, but I couldn't forgive myself if I didn't at least try."

She doesn't say any more after that.

"I'm sorry to hear all that, Angie. What can you tell me about them? What wa—" Penny catches himself, "—is Jon's friend's name?"

On the other end, Angie lets out another chuckle through her nose, this one a lot less good-natured than the first.

"It's alright. You're not the only one who thinks … who thinks …" she searches for the right words, "who thinks maybe they won't be coming back. I don't actually know. I've seen him around, but I never got his name. I just know that he and Jon used to work together before Jon became head pastor. They're close. They're together still, I'm sure of it."

"Hey, hey, don't sweat it, that's alright. Do you know where they worked together?"

She hesitates. "Yea, they were together at the Utah Geological Survey, both surveyors. That's where Jon discovered the Holy Stone in the Desert, where he …" she chokes up and composes herself all in one movement. She's rolled these feelings around her mind until their edges have nearly rubbed off. "… where he first got inspired to spread the word. They should have known better …" She trails off.

"OK, that's where I'll start then. One last question. What … uhh … what was your, you know, what was relationship to Jon? Like, I mean, was your relationship *just* church-based, or, did you do, like, non-church-based stuff together?" *Non-church-based stuff?!* "… you get what I'm asking."

Angie chuckles again. Those charming little exhales.

"Yes, detective. Though he was my pastor first, we also did 'non-church-based stuff,' as you said, together. We dated, in *adult* words. Not for long, though. And we had a friendly break-up a couple months ago."

Maybe she thought it was cute? Yea, she probably thought it was cute.

"Thanks, Angie. I'll get started on this now. Pro-bono. I could never charge for helping a church find its pastor. Can I call you here or do you have … another number?" Penny asks, tentatively.

"Nope, just this one. It's my cell. Call me if I can do anything. And Penny? Thank you."

"Surely. And if you need me, stop on by, or give me a call. Or both. I'm in the Airbnb just outside town that's shaped like half a Bucky-Fuller ball," before giving her his personal number.

Penny hangs up the phone and exhales for what feels like the first time in ten minutes. It may be the crystals hanging around the room, he isn't sure, but it seems like sunlight hangs in the air, suspended by a static charge. His heart beats and his stomach falls. He wants to call her back, but there's no reason. Doors swing wide open in the meat of his chest, as possibility blows through them, but he shuts them carefully, one by one. There's too much to do. He looks back at the phone, hoping the sight will bring him back to her sounds, but it doesn't. It's just an echo, an absence. He walks to the door.

The phone rings. He rushes back.

"Are you my son?" hollers an old man with a crazed twang.

"My guess is no? Mr. Jenkins?" he asks.

"Who? No! I'm Karl. Where's my son?"

"Karl … Stillman, by any chance?"

"No, goddamit! Stop asking me if I'm this guy or that guy, there's six thousand of us here. You'll be asking all damn day. I keep sending letters. No one ever writes back. My son would know." The old man stops, waiting for an answer to a question he didn't quite ask.

"Is your son missing by any chance, sir?"

"No! Or, maybe. I don't know. He's not missing, I just can't find him … Can you find him?"

Penny pauses. He's remembering an old Indigenous parable he heard at a spiritual retreat in Southern California. 'Know that everything is connected to everything.'

"Sure, Karl. I'll be right by. Where to?"

"The Silver Dollar Saloon. I'll be here all day. And the day after that. And the one after that one, and also, the one …"

The old man keeps going with this. Stuck in some sort of eternal recurrence. Penny hangs up the phone gingerly, hoping not to disturb the man any further.

Driving through Moab, he thinks about what Angie said—how 70 years ago, this was a frontier town for cowboys and excavators, marksmen and fossil hunters—as he tries to imagine what this long, thin strip of stores and cheap motels, like a strip of tape loosely clinging to the dirt and dust, looked like before. He drives past a kitschy rock shop loomed over by a giant yellow sign advertising dinosaur bones and minerals, and, for a moment, he sees it. No sign, no stands, no tourists. Just a man persistent as the planets on their axis, going out every day to scrape the corners of this blasted dirt furnace for the hidden bones of creatures long dead. His days and weeks and years of failure. His one glorious success. His sad sigh as the town changed, leaving him and his crookened back in the past.

He passes one, two, three motels sucking water and burning lights. All offering swimming pools and AC in the desert. He comes to a stop in front of the austere building of the Utah Geological Survey.

The door opens to a tiny little waiting area and faces a giant, steel keycard-secured door. Glass windows with little speaker boxes and gaps for handing notes are set into the walls on either side of the room. He turns left and makes eye contact with a woman who shakes her head and points the other way. Penny shrugs and disco spins back to the other window. A clearly well-loved spider plant hangs behind the second woman, long leaves suspended by hooks screwed into the ceiling.

"Can I help you, darling?" she asks in a friendly but tired voice.

"Yes, ma'am. Thank you, ma'am." Penny has begun speaking in a Southern accent. He stops this. "So, I'm looking for some records on an old employee who worked in the UGS, maybe three, four years ago? He's—"

She interrupts.

"You're looking for records then, love."

He pauses for a moment. Confused.

"Uh, yeah, that's what I'm saying, I'm looking for records on an old employee who—"

"No, you're looking for Records, the Division of Records, son. We can buzz you through."

He sees The Lady on the Right look over his shoulder at The Lady on the Left with a gleam in her eye. A grating buzzer sounds behind him, and The Lady on the Right speaks up again.

"Alright, there's your exit, hun. Walk down the hallway, about halfway, take the elevator down to B6—Records—and ask for Otto. Well, just tell Otto you're there for records. It's just him, anyways."

"Groovy. Thanks."

The hallway is made of white-painted cinder block, and framed clippings stick on particle boards that hang every few feet down the walls. They start with history from the 1910s—an original edition of the first geological survey of mining in Utah—and continue through to modern day clean-up efforts of radioactive mines on Navajo Nation territory. The 1940s display catches Penny's eye.

Apparently, starting in the 1900s, efforts to mine a periodic metal called vanadium accidentally led to uranium production as a by-product. The dirt was so tangled with minerals that if you scooped a cup of one, you came back with half a cup of the other.

At the time, no one cared. 'Sure, great, I guess we can sell this. Hell, we can sell anything,' said the original profiteers, not yet cloyingly embarrassed by their nature. But, a few years later, American scientists cracked open the soul of matter, discovering the smiling diplomat of death inside, the fission bomb, and American foreign policy would never be the same.

To fuel the chimera of Truman, Patton, and others, the United States needed an elemental metal happy to disintegrate: uranium. As the United States often does—in its interest, rarely in others'—it rigged the markets. In 1946, said the sign, the Atomic Energy Act made the U.S. government the sole purchaser of radioactive raw materials in the country, inflating the price of uranium, and setting off a Utah Gold Rush for our fizzy friend.

A picture of a grimacing man with no hair in a safari outfit, like a bald Teddy Roosevelt, holds prominent position in the display. Charles Steen, it says his name is. In 1952, he discovered the first and largest deposit of uranium just outside Moab whose proceeds he would proceed to waste for the next 16 years on dalliances like daily flights to Salt Lake City for salsa lessons, at which point he declared bankruptcy. The uranium trade died down in the 1980s, but some are hopeful that it's picking back up today.

Penny rides the elevator down to the bottom floor and enters a giant domed room with a giant round globe in the center of it. It feels like a planetarium. Dozens of computer racks twice a tall man's height stand in orderly rows on either side of the globe and seated behind a sleek silver monitor hunches a little man with round glasses pecking quickly at the keys.

"Otto? Is that you? Is this Records?" Penny asks.

"What? Who? Yes. Come, come, what do you want?" he says in heavily accented English.

"Uhh, I'm here for … uhh … records?"

"Yes. Already implied. What do you want?"

"I'm doing some looking on a case. Someone who used to work—hold on, sorry man, like, where are you from?"

"Ah. This? Yes. Always too obvious for me. The accent. I know. Los Alamos. New Mexico. Through Argentina. From … you can guess."

Otto doesn't want to say much more on this subject, it seems.

"Your friend?" Otto asks.

"Oh, yea. Maybe you know him? Jon Stillman?"

"Ahh, yes. Jon. Of course. Jon. He worked here, yes. A real field rat, him. Him and his friend, too." Otto winks.

"Yes! That's him. Or I think it's him, anyways. What can you tell me about them, the two of them, hopefully."

"Two very interesting boys. Certainly. Like any natural pairing. Complementary poles. Jon had ideas, *suggestions*. Karl had will, drive, action. They were out in the hills every day, looking, looking, looking. You could say they found what they were looking for."

"And what was that?"

"You tell me. Do you know what's in those hills?"

Penny didn't. He pauses for a moment, thinking.

"Uhh … gold?"

"What? Gold! What year do you think it is? No, not gold, uranium. *Uranium*. Sweet, precious uranium."

"You don't have to be mean about it."

Otto says nothing in response to this.

"Well, did they find it or didn't they?"

"I don't know exactly. It's too soon to say. But it's possible. Initial readings are promising. Come, come, look at this."

The little man leaps up excitedly, and rushes over, giving Penny no time to come anywhere. In his hand is a print-out with graphs and tables and parcel drawings of Moab. None of it makes any sense.

"Oh, you neanderthal. Yes. *Radioactivity*. Here. Again. This time, in town. Accessible. Under the Silver Dollar Saloon."

Synapses fire in concert like a daisy chain of lightbulbs passing charge down the line. Uranium. Silver Dollar Saloon. And then. Karl?

"Karl what, Otto? What was Jon's friends last name."

"Perdue, my sweet, stupid, boy."

"Karl Perdue? 5'11", 196 lbs, from Moab, Utah."

"Yes! Him! Look, colleagues, he does know something. But does he know who owns what? Who owes what? What does he know?"

Penny's eyes sharpen, just barely, it's possible Otto doesn't even notice. Then they slack again. Back to his usual wide-eyed gaze.

"Not much, I guess. More now. Muchas gracis, Otto."

Quickly, now, Penny rushes to the Silver Dollar Saloon. It's been mentioned not once, not twice, but three times on different threads in the mess of unrelated but deeply connected plots whose tangle makes up the world. There had been so many crazy energetic experiences since he started connecting with Moab as a space. The Saloon had to be one of them.

God, and what a building too. Old, old pine beams so weathered by sun and rain they'd faded grey; a long, waist-high railing outside that Mr. Jenkins's cowboys used to kick a foot up on after tying their horses to the posts a few feet into the street. It's a tall building, with huge white serif lettering declaring it the 'Silver Dollar Saloon' and smaller serif numbering dating it to 1879. Just inside the door, a wooden wall with frosted glass inlaid in the middle blocks the view of the rest of the bar through the swinging double doors. Some memory in the soup of Penny's mind tells him these were used to keep wives from seeing their drunk husbands inside. Another calls that explanation stupid and says it was to block the wind.

"Are you Karl?" Penny asks the old man sitting by the only phone in sight, using his powers of detection.

"Karl Sr., sir."

"Like, charmed, man. We talked earlier."

"Yes! But it's fine now. I found Karl Jr. He's in the back making burgers. Not to worry! He explained everything."

Penny feels a little bad for this old man. Who knows what he was like before.

"Well, can you explain it to me, sir? Sometimes I just need an explanation, about anything, and everything just clears right up."

"I'd been sending the checks, for the Saloon—you know, even buildings gotta pay the tax man—but no one ever wrote me back. They used to! They'd write me back every time. But not anymore. They didn't write me back for a year. And Jr, see, he'd send the letters, so I thought he knew. And it turns out he did. He was gone, but he got back. They're doing it online now. *Online.* I don't know online!"

"Can I see Karl ... Karl?"

"Sure! Now that he's back feel free. Feel free to go back there. He's in the kitchen."

Walking toward the kitchen, a universal synchronicity whispers something quiet into Penny's ear. Synchronicity is a funny thing. Sometimes, it's a comet lighting your way out of the forest, other times it's a trail of four-leafed clovers ending in a fresh spring. This time it was the ring of his cell phone.

"Penny? It's Angie, I'm back at your place. I have something I need to tell you."

In a flash, he shows up at the Airbnb, letting in Angie, who's standing by the door.

"So, what is it?" he asks.

Angie stares around at the decorations, not so much looking at them as preparing herself to talk.

She takes a few deep breaths and then stands completely still.

"I knew them both, Penny. I knew Jon and Karl."

Penny waits for her to continue.

"I didn't tell you because I wanted you to find them without me. We're … involved in something."

"Couldn't be the property sale, could it?" Penny asks.

Her eyes open wide in alarm.

"How do you—"

He freezes as if he doesn't know how to answer, then he points at the classifieds section of the newspaper. There, in bold letters is the mandatory notice for any tax sale: Delinquent Notice; Immediate Sale. Today. 315 Harrison Ave, Moab, UT; a.k.a. Silver Dollar Saloon.

"I never took you for a current events guy."

"There's just one event I'm current on."

"Then, I don't need to tell you anything."

He walks around to the table, and gestures to both chairs.

"Indulge me."

"Well. Fine. Karl Jr. took over the property tax payments for his dad at the Saloon, a year ago. That's how little time it takes. One payment, missed one year, and they can take your house. We figured … we figured we could take the Saloon, not change a thing. They weren't supposed to go out there and die. What am I supposed to tell Karl Sr. if I take the bar now? It's just you and me, Karl, don't worry about the money, I'll take care of it. You know me. Oh, you don't? Well, anyways, don't worry about it."

"Wait, hold on. I've got some good news," and Penny smiles. But not his usual vacant smile. A sharper smile, more sinister. "Karl Jr's not dead. I found him a few days ago. I didn't know who he was then, but he's back at the bar, safe and sound." He waits to let the moment sink in.

"He's alive? That son-of-a-bitch. He hasn't said a damn thing and the sale is today. Wait. OK. What about Jon, then? Did you find him too?"

"Nope, just Karl," Penny says, too happy for the message he's delivering. "Karl said this was their victory lap out there in the desert. Victory lap is what he said."

"He was covered in blood when I found him. Like, he'd been in a fight and just barely made it out. You don't think he maybe, like, killed Jon do you?'

"No, he wouldn't. He ..." She closes her eyes and breathes deep. "Yes, I suppose I do think that. Goddamit, he must have."

Penny shakes his head, but he can't quit the grin. Angie's eyes fill with rage. She looks both directions and goes running from the room.

There's only one place to go, Penny knows. Good luck, finally, it all seems. He's pulling up to the Saloon now, and the sun hangs high and red in the air. The red silt from the town's famous arches has blown into the street and now spins in whorls through the air. Karl's walking through the swinging doors. They clamor back together on the other side of his torso.

Out in the dirt on the street in front of the Saloon, a few men in suits—certainly bureaucrats—sit behind a table that looms over two rows of empty folding chairs. On each chair is a bidding paddle. The tax sale has come and it looks like a hanging.

Her long shadow trailing behind her like a veil, Angie is pulling a six shooter from her pocket, as Karl Jr. comes down the stairs. The sounds of a tambor thumping like a heartbeat, and the high whistle of a cowboy shootout float out from the public radio playing in Penny's car.

Next door, Mr. Jenkins notices this before anyone else. He gasps, and drops a sack of grain, which explodes as it hits the deck.

The auctioneers scream when they see Angie. Karl Jr., feet now planted square on the dirt, standing just twenty paces away from the woman with the gun, reaches for his hip as quick as he can. He understands immediately. *She knows*. And he'd been expecting this.

Two shots ring out, the shadows jolt, and then stay still, for a brief second. One shadow wavers as a body falls to meet it. Karl Jr. lies dead and pandemonium explodes.

"She shot him!" yells an auctioneer.

Mr. Jenkins begins whooping. Karl Sr. tries to speak but can only scratch out a cry. He's just watched his son die.

"Put the gun down, ma'am" yells a woman Penny recognizes as a patron of the

Outlaw Café, one too-large handgun in each hand and one watermelon-sized sheriff's badge pinned to her chest. "Come with me."

Within a half hour, the dust has settled, and the tax auction picks up again. Angie has been taken to jail. Karl Sr. rode away with his son's corpse. Jon remains lost, almost certainly dead, in the desert. But one bidder remains.

The Silver Dollar Saloon, a property appraised at $850,000, sitting on what will eventually be known as the second-largest deposit of uranium in the State of Utah—to be valued at $70,000,000—is hammered down at auction for a final price of $19,000 to one Penn Spellman, otherwise known as Penny, agent and investigator for the Stonefield Investment Group.

A few weeks later, back in Montvale, New Jersey, at Stonefield's headquarters, investigators trade stories about property tax investments they've made over the past months. Each one describing how they turned the temporary misfortune of homeowners or their unintentional lapse in vigilance into a profit by paying extremely sub-market rates for homes sold at auction, and immediately flipping them. Some homes were bought for $10,000 and sold for $200,000 the very next day. One investigator describes his strategy as trying to catch homeowners unaware. None are particularly concerned with the ethics of the situation.

"Oh yea? You bought 35 in Philly? Those are kiddie numbers. You'll never get anywhere like that. I've been buying up vacants in Pittsburgh and pitching them as new rental units to overseas investors. Just switch the pictures online, use the money from the first investor to pay the next one, and these Brazilians never know the difference."

"That sounds a lot like a Ponzi scheme, right?"

A third voice chimes up.

"Yea, like almost exactly like a Ponzi scheme."

"What are you guys? Cops? Who cares as long as we're getting ours."

They laugh in unison. One of them lowers their voice conspiratorially.

"Hey, so did you guys hear what Penn did?"

"Yea, that's one cold operator, man."

"I heard he killed a guy in the desert, and then killed another guy in town for his last gig."

"Well, I heard he was stealing the owner's tax checks to put him under."

"I heard he's been working on this one for 20 years. Didn't he live out there once?"

"Cold operator, man."

"Ask me, I can't ever tell if he's Penny or Penn."

"Don't be stupid. It's an act. That's how he gets people."

"Neither? Both? Two-faced like a penny."

"You make a face like that long enough and it gets stuck, you know."

"Why don't you guys, like, ask me?"

Penny walks up, vacant eyed and smiling. Suddenly, his eyes are sharp like a raptor's and the smile falls. All three flinch. Penny smiles again and walks away.

THE CASE OF THE BEGUILED COURIER

J. R. Lindermuth

"If I thought it was him I'd break his arm," Max said.

The man doesn't mince words. I must have smirked because he glared at me. "What? You don't think I could do it? When I was in the kibbutz I learned Krav Maga."

Max is five-two and as wide as he is tall. A lot of years have passed since he was in a kibbutz but I doubt if he was any more aggressive then than he is now. So I had my doubts about him learning the Israeli self-defense system. Still, he was as steamed up as I'd ever seen him, so I didn't express my skepticism.

I'm a private detective. I used to be a cop and the diamond district was part of my turf. I got to know the people and they've learned to trust me as much as they trust any outsider. So, when I started the business, I offered them my services and it's been lucrative. These people believe in security and they're not shy about paying for it.

"I think you should start from the beginning, Max. What happened and what do you want me to do about it?"

"I want the diamonds back and, if you can manage it, I want you should catch the damned thief and hand him over to the cops." Max is one of the best diamond cutters in the district and he moves some quality stones.

"How did this thief get the diamonds?"

"That's for you to figure out. I locked the stones in a briefcase. Irv took them to Zechman. Only when they opened the case, the stones were gone."

"The briefcase was empty?"

"That's what I'm telling you."

Word was the diamonds hadn't been offered up in the district. It seemed likely the thief was waiting for things to cool down before trying to dispose of them.

"Do you think Irv stole them?"

"What, are you crazy? Irv is my brother-in-law. He's no thief. He's been transporting stones for me for years, never lost a one before."

I know Irv and I didn't think he was a thief either. But people do change, no matter how long you've known them or trusted them. "What did Irv say? Did he stop somewhere along the way? He might have set the case down for a minute, long enough for someone to tamper with it"

"He insists he didn't stop nowhere."

"How did the thief know he was carrying diamonds?"

Max gave me a look. "What, are you stupid, Harry? You spot a guy down here with a briefcase chained to his wrist you think he's transporting bagels? People talk. They gossip. Everybody knows everybody's business."

"I hate to ask, him being your brother-in-law and all. Do you think Irv might have developed some bad habits you don't know about? Like gambling, or women, or …"

Max scowled. "Irv ain't got no bad habits. He don't gamble. He's got my sister, so he don't need no women on the side. I trust him with my goods. He's the courier I trust. He's never given me cause to think he'd stab me in the back."

"Well, I think I should talk to him anyway. Where is he?"

"I sent him home. He's upset. He thinks I'm mad at him. I'm not. I'm mad at the crook what stole the stones. You go talk to him. He'll tell you what I already did."

In contrast to his brother-in-law who is short and fat, Irv is tall and skinny. If he played the game, he could drop a basketball through the hoop without needing to jump or stretch. I found him on his sofa, elbows propped on his knees and chin cupped in his hands, a morose frown darkening his mug.

"Cheer him up, Harry," his wife Nadine said. "Tell him it wasn't his fault." She offered me babka and tea as an inducement. Even if I wasn't inclined to do as she asked, I'd have been tempted. This woman's food is a blessing.

While I nibbled the goodies and sipped the brew I tried talking Irv out of his despondency. "Max isn't blaming you. He knows you wouldn't steal from him. He's hired me to try and track down the thief. But I need your help."

"How can I help? I don't know what happened."

"Tell me what you did—from the time you left the shop until you got to Zechman's."

Irv swept a big hand across his brow. "That's what's so troubling, Harry. I remember leaving the shop and I arrived at Zechman's. But I don't know nothing about what happened in between."

I arched an eyebrow. "How can that be? You gotta know how you got there."

"But I don't," he said with a sigh.

My next stop was Zechman's cramped little shop which, contrary to the majority of diamantaires, is located outside the boundaries of the district. He haggles with jewelers and other buyers from around the world and has depended on Max for his polishing and cutting for years. There's trust between the two men, and Max is the only reason Zechman deigns to speak to me.

Unfortunately, he had nothing more to tell me than I already knew.

"Irv showed up as he always does," he said. "But he was late—for the first time ever. That was irritation enough. Then he opened the case and it was empty. The stones were gone and that buffoon couldn't tell what happened to them."

"You're not blaming Max, are you?"

He glared at me with a look that could have singed wallpaper. "Of course not. I'd trust Max with my life. He's been cutting my stones for years."

"I guess those stones represent a lot of money?"

Zechman scowled. "Don't ask."

I didn't. Instead, I inquired how Irv had come to the shop.

Zechman shrugged his narrow shoulders. "A taxi, I suppose. Like always. I didn't see."

When you need information I've learned the best source is often your local bartender. Shirley's place is also outside the district but near enough to garner trade from those who frequent it and news of what happens there-in. Shirley is not a gossip but rather a purveyor of news—or, so she's told me often enough.

Her reporting has often benefited my enterprise. I was all ears when I asked if she knew anything of Irv's loss of the diamonds entrusted to him.

Shirley pursed her lips and glanced around to assure no one eavesdropped on our conversation. Then she poured me another drink and leaned close across the bar. "I hate to tell you this, sport," she whispered in her booze-husky voice. "Our buddy Irv has picked up a bad habit. He's got in the habit of stopping at a certain bistro when Max sends him on a mission. He's become infatuated with a girl what works there."

I was shocked. "He's cheating on Nadine?"

"Nah. From what I hear, the most he does is guzzle coffee and ogle the girl. She's a real looker and has him under her spell. He'd probably jump off a roof if she asked him to do it. But she's not looking for any kind of relationship with him, far as I can tell.

"This girl used to be an LPN until some pharmaceuticals went missing. The hospital couldn't pin it on her but they wouldn't keep her on either. So now she slings coffee and sandwiches at this place. She has a lover, a real hard case what drives a taxi, and might be into some other stuff if you get my drift."

Sheepishly, his head bowed and his face flushed scarlet, Irv confessed his attraction to the girl when we met later at my office. It wasn't a tale he'd want to tell in Nadine's presence.

"She's beautiful, Harry. I've never seen a girl so beautiful as Lucy. I stopped for a coffee one day and the sight of her took my breath away. I couldn't help myself. I had to go back. Again. And again. She's like a drug, Harry. I can't get enough of seeing her and listening to her talk.

"But that's all it is. I swear, Harry. You know me. I would never cheat on Nadine. I just stop for coffee, feast my eyes on her for a little while, and then I go on my way, the rest of my day made brighter just from the pleasure of looking."

"Did you stop to see her the day you lost the diamonds?"

Irv chewed his bottom lip and mulled the possibility. "I don't remember. I probably did though. I don't get much chance to go out except when I make my courier runs. Max keeps me pretty busy in the shop otherwise."

"Do you think you might have taken her boyfriend's cab when you left the restaurant?"

He considered, nibbling a fingernail. "Maybe. I don't remember. I could have. He did take me other times."

Irv's confession prompted the beginning of an idea of what might have happened to those stones. It seemed clear to me Irv must have been drugged since he was foggy about what happened between the time he left the shop and his arrival at Zechman's. I wasn't sure exactly how it was done. But given the object of his affection had been a nurse and knew about drugs it made her a prime suspect.

If I was to recover the stones or at least collar the thieves I needed to do a little research first. Having been on the job for as long as I had gave me a distinct advantage in that respect. I knew a lot of people and many owed me favors. It was time to collect.

My first stop was a doctor I kept out of jail. I won't mention his crime. It was serious enough but he promised to go straight and provided information that put several worse people behind bars. Sure, I could have arrested him too. Yet, it's always good to have something for leverage when you need certain kinds of help. Doc kept his word and his help is always available when needed.

My contact informed me there were some anesthetic-type drugs like scopolamine, diazepam, midazolam, and others that could induce temporary amnesia.

"Midazolam, for instance, doesn't knock a patient out," he explained. "It just makes them sleepy. The sedation can last for up to six hours and, often, the patient has no memory of what goes on while they're out."

"My subject doesn't remember being injected," I told him.

"It can be injected. It can also be given by mouth, intravenously, or by spraying up the nose."

A light dawned. "So, it might be given in a cup of coffee or other drink?"

"Sure. Patient probably wouldn't even notice a difference in taste of the beverage."

"How long does it take to start working?"

"Usually, no more than 15 minutes or so."

A former nurse would have no problem slipping such a drug into the coffee of a guy besotted with her looks. I decided it was time I had a cup of coffee.

Irv was right. She was a looker. Not the most gorgeous woman I've ever seen, though lovely enough to grab the attention of any red-blooded man. No offense to Nadine, who is a kind and gracious woman and a wonderful cook but not a stunner in the looks department, but I could understand how this Lucy had beguiled Irv.

She had big blue eyes, a mane of honey-gold hair, and curves in all the right places. I sat, drinking my coffee, following her sensuous movements like all the other men in the restaurant. I'd noticed right off there wasn't another woman in the place. Lucy had no competition; she had us all to herself and was rewarded with hefty tips. She was friendly and attentive to all her customers, yet officious in her manner if you were paying attention. Still, unlike some of the others who were as enamored as Irv, I realized her smile for every man was accompanied by a malevolent gleam in her eye. It was something you had to be quick to catch, but it was definitely there.

I was on my second cup of coffee, gazing with delight like the others when the boyfriend came in. His appearance didn't measure up to hers. He was a skinny little guy with a pinched face like a weasel. Still, it was clear she saw something in him that wasn't apparent to the rest of us. Lucy threw her arms around him, planted a lingering kiss on his lips, then stood rapt with attention as he whispered words in her sweet ear.

I left a tip and took my leave. I had other places to go.

I have no legal authority to seek subpoenas or make arrests. So, I took my suspicions to my friend and ex-partner Jim Reilly at the precinct where I used to work. Jim listened with interest. He was familiar with the case. Max and Zechman had reported the theft, though the detective assigned had made no headway on the investigation. Jim told me something else I found interesting. Lucy was Zechman's niece.

"Who told you that?"

"Who do you think?" Jim said. "Our mutual friend Shirley. The woman knows everything about everyone. Besides, who do you think put up her bail when the girl was pulled in on that hospital investigation?"

Jim agreed to follow up on the subpoenas I'd suggested.

Lucy's boyfriend cracked after more of the drug used on Irv was found in the apartment they shared. Jim said the guy's confession prompted a barrage of words he never expected to hear coming out of Lucy's pretty mouth.

It seems Lucy was the one who came up with the scheme. Her uncle was experiencing some financial difficulties and she convinced him stealing the stones would benefit all three of them. She drugged Irv, and her boyfriend hustled him out to his cab and took him to Zechman's shop. There they were able to open the case and lift the stones. After reporting the theft to police, Zechman filed an insurance claim. Later, when things cooled down, the plan was to sell the gems in the foreign market.

"Why, Zechman?" I asked at the station after he and his partners were taken into custody.

"Why else?" he said with a shrug. "I needed cash. I over-extended and then the economy went sour. We figured we could get away with it and nobody would get hurt."

"Irv got hurt. Max got hurt. I thought Max was your friend?"

He shrugged again. "There are friends. And then there's money. You gotta do what you gotta do."

I SMELL A MYSTERY

Adrienne Stevenson

Me and Terry—my twin sister—were cleaning out Aunt Martha's place last week. The old girl up and died just after she moved into one of them retirement apartments across town. After the funeral, her lawyer called and asked if Ma could go through her things, since the Will said she could take whatever she wanted from the house. Auntie's lawyer wanted it cleared this week, so the agent could list it. Something about getting the will probated.

As far as Ma's concerned, we could shovel everything into a dumpster.

Terry said we should go and see what we might find. See, Aunt Martha—she was Ma's aunt, really—was a hoarder her whole life. You know how it is with hoarders—most of it's junk, but now and then there's a treasure or two. So we rode our bikes over to Auntie's house.

We scouted around the bungalow. Stuff crammed everywhere. Mountains of magazines and papers, shelves of knick-knacks and books, and dishes and cans hiding the kitchen counters. Nothing compared to the basement though. Boxes of jars, shelves of pickles dating back ten years, stacks of scrap lumber, a work bench piled with unfinished bird-houses and feeders; tubs of birdseed, piles of old towels, curtains, more dusty magazines. Sure didn't look like much of a prospect for treasure.

Terry said I should do the basement and she'd take the upstairs. I was happy to skip the smells of old slippers and sour milk. Not that I had a choice after Terry decided. Sometimes she's so bossy. She's only fifteen minutes older than me. After fourteen years, what are a few minutes?

At least the basement was cool. But it smelled funny, too, like damp cement and open sump-pumps. I noticed a cubby-hole filled with old sheets, near the furnace. The smell over there knocked me back. Kind of sweet and sour, like a forgotten piece of meat on the counter.

I pulled on an edge of blanket and a cold yellowish hand flopped out. I'm no sissy, but I screamed.

Next thing I know there's Terry, clomping downstairs and yelling "What's wrong? Are you hurt?" The hand stopped her in her tracks.

"C'mon, Arlie, leave it alone. We've got to call Ma, or 911, or something." She took my hand and dragged me up the stairs.

Terry decided she'd better call Ma first, since the hand, and whatever it was attached to, was obviously dead. Ma hollered a bit—Terry held the phone away from her head—but eventually calmed down and said to call emergency services and she'd try to get off early.

Terry made the call and we both put our ears to the phone. The man who answered at 911 sounded skeptical, but after some muttering he said he would send over a patrol car, and we'd better not be fooling around because the officers would take it unkindly if we were.

"Let's wait outside," I said.

Before long, a cop cruiser pulled up by the house. Two uniformed officers got out and came up the front walk. A man, the usual Hulk type, and a woman, even taller than he was, with more stripes on her uniform.

"Are you the girls who called about a body?" asked the man. We said we were.

The woman pitched in. Her voice sounded like she'd been gargling with rocks. "Can you show us?"

We led the way to the basement. When we got to the bottom of the stairs, Terry hung back a bit so I had to show them the place behind the furnace. "I found it, ma'am," I said.

"And your name is?"

"Arlette Peters, ma'am. Mostly go by Arlie."

"Is this exactly as you found it, Arlie?"

"Yes'm," I said. "We know about not disturbing bodies, from the crime scene shows on TV."

"You did the right thing. Now," she looked me up and down, "you leave the rest to us. We'll be in touch with your mother."

We rode home slowly, not talking much. It was a relief to get where the only smell came from pot roast in the slow cooker. Even our normal clutter looked pretty bare after Auntie's place.

I asked Ma at dinner if she knew who the body could be. She said she had no idea.

Next morning, the cops came around to our place. Gravel-voice—Sergeant Cooper—was there, with a white-haired man in street clothes, an Inspector. They said they were treating this as a suspicious death. Then he questioned each of us alone in the living room.

I went first, since I found the body.

It was all pretty low-key, not like they show it on TV. I said my piece like I did the day before.

The Inspector showed me a picture of a face. An old man, with short grey hair, bushy eyebrows and buck-teeth that stuck out a bit even with his mouth closed. It had been prettied up some, but you could still tell it was a dead person. "Have you ever seen him?" I shook my head.

"Did your aunt have many visitors?" he asked. I explained about how we hardly had anything to do with her. He sent me outside to wait for the others.

Soon, Terry came and joined me at the picnic table in our back yard, and Ma came to collect us not long after. She said they'd be finished with Auntie's place by the end of the day, so we could go back tomorrow, if we wanted.

Terry and I looked at each other. Ma laughed. "It's OK, they cleaned out the cubby hole. Probably disinfected it, too. Nobody told me about any buried treasure in with the body, either."

So there we were, next day, back at Aunt Martha's, turning out cupboards & sorting through stacks of stuff. I felt kind of flat, as if there should have been more excitement. I wasn't keen to go back in the basement, either, in spite of what Ma said. So I told Terry I'd help her with upstairs and she could help me with the basement. She teased me about being a fraidy-cat as we worked, until I shoved her, hard.

Terry slipped on a magazine and lost her balance. Damn if she didn't crash into a whole pile of books sitting in the middle of the floor, and fall half-under them. I reached a hand to help and she pulled me down with her. We rolled around a bit, wrestling, then got the giggles and had to stop.

Some of the books had fallen open. One didn't look like a regular book. It was handwritten. "Whoa, Terry, get a load of this. Somebody's diary."

I started to read out loud.

May 5, 1962

Jack married Norma today. Good catering. Nancy was flower girl, too old if you ask me but nobody ever does. Stu showed up for the meal but not the church. He got drunk on the punch.

"Jack? Our grandfather? Cool! We have to take it to show Ma." said Terry. "I wonder if that's the only one." I checked for the last date. October 30, 1975. There must be more. Finally, something interesting to look for.

"Hey! Pictures!" Terry held up an old-style photo album. I had a quick look, then we both started to search harder. By lunch-time we had a stack of five diaries and eight photo albums. I had found a couple of old books I thought might be worth something, too. Terry pooh-poohed that, of course. I figured it would fit in the carriers on our bikes. And we had sure made some mess. Books and papers lay around everywhere. No more neat stacks. I wondered if Auntie had some kind of secret organizing system, but it was too late to tell.

Her kitchen didn't turn up anything interesting to eat. Stale crackers and peanut butter that had gone hard around the edges? No thanks. We figured it was better to take our loot home and have something decent there. And come back later.

Only it didn't quite turn out the way we planned.

We turned into Aunt Martha's street around two o'clock, and could tell something was wrong right away. There were people standing in the street, gawking, and smoke pouring out of the house. A fire truck passed us, siren screaming.

"I thought you locked up," said Terry.

"I did, front and back," I said. "I double-checked."

"We didn't leave any lights on, did we?"

"Nope."

We watched as the fire crew broke through the door and sprayed water all over.

"If there were any books worth saving, they won't be now," I said.

A cop cruiser joined the fire truck, and our old friend Sergeant Cooper got out. She looked around at the crowd. Should we stay, or go? No decision—she'd spotted us, and waved us over.

"You girls know what happened here?"

"We just got back from lunch, ma'am. It was fine when we left this morning. All locked up and powered down, ma'am," said Terry. Cooper raised an eyebrow, then nodded and scanned the crowd again. "Forced entry and arson," she muttered to herself, scowling. "No reason to think otherwise. And that place was set to go up like tinder." She turned back to us. "You might as well go home, kids, you won't be allowed back in for a while."

Ma was some upset to hear about the fire. Once she calmed down a bit, she was interested in the diaries and albums, and agreed to go over them with us. We got them in order by date. There were a few gaps, but it looked like we had most of them.

The first diary started in 1956. Martha's Ma, our great-grandma, had written "Happy Sweet 16" in the front. The two of us looked over Ma's shoulders as she flipped pages. Mostly doodles in the first few pages, then entries at odd times, sometimes weeks apart, sometimes daily for a few days. Around 1958 she started writing about Stu, her first "grown-up" boyfriend. They met when she started work at the shoe factory. From then to about 1964 he showed up on every page. Then he disappeared. Martha skipped the whole last half of that year. When she started up again, part way through 1965, no more Stu.

"Did Aunt Martha ever marry?" I asked.

"No," said Ma, "at least, not as far as I remember. She'd have been thirty when I was born, and she never said much about the past. Neither did my Pa, and I never even met my Aunt Nancy. She ran off with someone, I think."

"Aunt Nancy? How come we never even heard of her?" Me and Terry were both gob-smacked.

"Like I said, nobody talked about the past."

Ma kept turning pages, and we moved from book to book. In 1980 the shoe factory shut down. Aunt Martha took a secretarial job with the town, preparing papers and minutes of council meetings. After she retired, she took in a boarder to help with expenses. She bought her house when houses really were affordable, not like now when Ma has to scrape to pay the mortgage. Auntie only stopped taking boarders when she got her old age pension. The last entry in the last book talked about missing both the cash and the company. That was back in 2010. It's now 2013.

"I wonder if she kept on with it after this," said Ma.

"If she did, and it's in the house, it'll be useless now," Terry said. "Everything got soaked by the fire hoses."

"What about the pictures?" I asked. "Maybe there's something there. I'd like to see a picture of Aunt Nancy, and that Stu guy."

Ma picked up the first album. It went all the way back to Aunt Martha's baby pictures, blurry and faded, in black and white. All the pictures were labelled. Good thing, because Ma didn't recognize many faces.

There were school pictures, family outings, special occasions. Several photos showed three kids on some steps. Martha at the bottom, then Jack, with Nancy at the top, so their heads came out even. I could see the Auntie I knew in young Martha's face. Nancy looked a lot like Martha. I looked over at Terry. We both did, too, especially around the nose and eyes. Now that I noticed, so did Ma. We all had curly hair, too. I shivered, like someone stepped on my grave. It was kind of scary, to think we would age like that.

Ma turned a few more pages. We all saw it the exact same moment. "It's that guy—the dead guy!" Terry said. Even though this face was younger, not to mention alive, it was the same person. Hard to mistake those eyebrows, or the teeth. He was smiling, showing off the buckteeth, and had his arm around Aunt Martha. Who at that point was nobody's aunt, I guess.

So ... the dead guy in Aunt Martha's house was Stu. But, Stu Who? Neither the diary or the labels gave his last name. Ma said we should call the cops, now that we had something to tell them. She went off to the kitchen to do that while Terry and I kept looking at the pictures.

Something about the later ones didn't seem quite right. I squinted hard, trying to figure out what it was. "That's not Martha with Stu—that's Nancy!"

Terry whistled. "I wonder how Martha felt about her boyfriend flirting with her sister. Anything about it in the diaries?"

"No. Say, didn't Ma say Nancy ran off with someone? Maybe Stu?"

"Nancy would have been ... what ... sixteen? Almost jailbait, like us."

Ma came back and said she had to take the diaries and photo albums down to the station in the morning.

"Aw, Ma, just when it was getting interesting," said Terry.

"We can take down some information and start searching on the web," I said. "Just because we don't have the originals doesn't mean we can't investigate. Remember that woman who talked to our class about family history? Can we photocopy some pictures, Ma? Please?"

Ma let us use her printer to copy pictures of Martha and Nancy and Stu, and we took down some dates from Martha's diaries that looked useful. First thing we did was search the internet for the people whose names we knew, and places they had worked or gone to school. Then we called up some family history sites, and it was there we struck pay dirt. Turns out we had some skeletons in our closet, sure as Auntie had a dead body in her basement.

"I can see why nobody ever talked about this," said Ma. She looked like she didn't know whether to laugh or cry. "To think, Auntie married, was expecting a child, then her sister ran off with her husband before the baby came. I guess everyone just wanted to forget the whole thing."

"But what happened to the baby, then?" I asked.

Ma shrugged. "I don't know," she said. "Maybe it died. Maybe it was put up for adoption."

"Maybe the cops will be able to get at the records," said Terry. "Won't there be some?"

"Yes," said Ma, "but in 1964 ... we didn't have anywhere near the paperwork on everyone we do now. There were plenty of laws, but people found loopholes. At least the birth was registered. She used the name 'Kandler'. So let's look up Stuart Kandler."

Long story short, Stu was a serial bigamist, and had been married already when he met Martha. After he "married" Nancy, he left her for someone else. No shortage of motive.

The cops thought so too, and they started a hunt for Stu's ex-wives. Ex-widows? We were more interested in finding out if Nancy was still alive, and what happened to Martha's child. That was on the cops' agenda too, but a lower priority.

The fire investigation took a couple of days, then we were allowed back into Martha's house. Ma brought over some fans, and we opened all the windows to try to get some air we could breathe.

The main floor was a write-off with masses of soggy paper and cardboard. Yuck. All we could do was shovel it—literally—into garbage bags and drag them outside. After a couple of hours, we went down to the basement.

"Let's box the recycle stuff and bag the rest for garbage," Terry suggested.

I nodded, and went upstairs to search for the garbage bags. Couldn't remember where I'd left them. As I passed the bathroom door, an arm reached out, a hand clapped over my mouth as the other arm held me round my waist. I struggled to escape.

"You're not going to scream, are you?" a voice whispered. A knife held in the other hand swung up and poked under my chin. I shook my head. The hand slowly lowered from my mouth, gripped my shoulder and turned me around.

It was like looking into a time-warped mirror.

"Aunt Nancy?" I whispered.

She relaxed, lowered the knife, and released me. I should have run.

"Aunt?" she said. "I suppose I must be. But you're so young. As young as I was, when ... I must be your great-aunt. So ... are you Jack's, or Martha's granddaughter?"

"Jack was our grandfather."

"Our? There's more than one?"

"My sister's in the basement." I should have kept my big mouth shut. Maybe Terry could have jumped her.

Nancy gripped my arm again, the knife in her other hand. "Let's go surprise her too."

I thumped my feet as loud as I dared going downstairs, but Terry was busy rooting around in some boxes.

"Come have a look at this, Arlie," she said, then raised her head as she lifted a wrapped object out of a box. "Oh! Who ...?"

"Terry, meet Aunt Nancy," I said. I tilted my head down towards the knife. Terry's eyes widened.

"What a surprise!" said Terry, with a big smile, stepping forward.

Nancy scowled, then sagged, and slumped down on the bottom step. "Nothing ever goes right," she moaned. And started to cry. Me and Terry could only watch. She was blocking our exit. It was embarrassing to see an old woman break down like that. I could feel myself turning red in sympathy.

"If you put the knife down, we can all go outside and talk," said Terry. "Would you like that?"

All her fight gone, Aunt Nancy nodded, and tossed the knife onto the floor. We followed her up the stairs, and took up our familiar seat on the front steps.

And then the cavalry came. OK, not the cavalry, but our old pal Sergeant Cooper, along with her partner, the Hulk. Turns out she had located Nancy and been tracking her movements. I admit, I felt a lot safer with Cooper there. Who knew what other weapon Nancy might have on her?

Turns out Nancy was Stu's last living "wife". Martha's daughter had died of influenza as a baby. Nancy had kept tabs on Stu, and when she found out he was planning to visit Martha, thought it about time she paid a visit to Martha herself. She and Martha had made up when along comes Stu and tries to stir the pot again. They were standing in the kitchen arguing, when Martha gave Stu a shove knocking him down to the back door landing. Nancy said Martha almost had a seizure on the spot, when they saw he was dead.

"Why wouldn't you just report his death?" said Cooper.

"You wouldn't have believed it was an accident," said Nancy. "We hid him behind the furnace. Martha said she'd make over the deed to me. She went on with her plans to move 'cause she was too old to do for herself and too ornery to live with me." Nancy's tears started again. "She was only seventy-three."

Cooper took Aunt Nancy's arm and gently helped her into the back of the cruiser. They drove off and left us.

Ma says the cops are charging Aunt Nancy with concealing a body. She could get off with a suspended sentence. Aunt Martha's lawyer says the papers deeding the house to Aunt Nancy should go through without a hitch. Nancy seems a lot friendlier than Martha, as long as we keep her away from knives.

The best part? Terry's basement find was a complete set of Limoges china that Ma had appraised for $10,000. And those two books I found? A signed first edition of *Anne of Green Gables* and an unsigned first of *The Wizard of Oz,* valued even higher than the china, around $12,000. So we both have starter funds for college.

Ma read this story and says with my grammar I need more than a starter fund.

I think that stinks.

A BAD HARE DAY

A You-Solve-It by John M. Floyd

"A man in a bunny suit?" Fran Valentine said, from the passenger seat.

Sheriff Lucy Valentine—Fran's daughter and only child—steered her cruiser off the highway and onto a long, private driveway lined with pear trees. "Yep. You know Frederic Wentworth, right? The bunny was hired to perform for Wentworth's five-year-old son's birthday party."

Lucy had received the phone call fifteen minutes ago, as she and her mother sat in the heat of the sheriff's office—the building's A/C was out as usual, and it was an unseasonably hot, steamy day. According to the call, the costumed performer had burglarized the wealthiest home in the county and gotten clean away.

"Got a riddle for you," Fran said, as they parked at the crime scene. "What did one rabbit say to the other?"

Lucy cut the engine and opened her door. "Let's see ... quit telling me stupid jokes?"

"No," she said, unfazed. "'Don't worry—be hoppy.'"

The sheriff groaned and said, as she headed toward the house, "I'll be hoppy. You wait for me in the car." Fran of course climbed out and followed.

They found Frederic Wentworth standing in the huge back yard of the country mansion where the party'd been held. In a dark suit soaked with sweat—Fran had never seen Wentworth in anything but a business suit—he told them several thousand dollars had been stolen from a cashbox in his den sometime during the birthday festivities earlier, and in fact the last of the party guests had just left, along with his wife and son. Lucy asked the appropriate questions, and twenty minutes later, following a search of the property, she and Fran and Wentworth made a surprising discovery. They found the performer, a big guy bound and gagged and blindfolded in the pool house closet underneath a stack of inflatable orange lifejackets.

When untied, the guy informed them he'd been whacked on the head from behind just before the party, and his rabbit costume was taken. Unfortunately he hadn't seen his attacker and could offer no description. More questioning proved fruitless, and after a while the hapless performer was paid, both for his time and for his lost costume, and was allowed to call his wife for a ride home. The sheriff and her mother and Wentworth, also hapless, reconvened inside the cool house.

They had only one lead: Wentworth felt certain there could be only three suspects in the crime.

"A team of yardworkers," he said. "They were the only ones besides me and my family and our guests who were on the property at the time."

Lucy said, "And they are now where?"

"Unfortunately all three left before I called you. At that time I thought the man I hired to do the bunny tricks was the robber. Wherever he was."

"Didn't you know he was still somewhere close by? When he left just now he called for a ride—didn't someone also drop him off, beforehand?"

"Yes, but there's thick woods behind the house. I thought he might've escaped on foot."

All of them fell silent. Outside the living-room windows, a landscaped front lawn sweltered in the sun.

At last Lucy said, "I still don't see how you can be so sure the impostor-thief was one of the yardworkers. It could've been one of your party guests."

Wentworth shook his head. "None of the guests had access to the house. My wife wanted it that way. Refreshments and bathrooms were available, but they were in the pool house." He paused and added, "Besides, the three workers were out of sight in the side yard during most of the party, and the den—where the cashbox was—is on that side of the house too, and I found one of its windows open. That'd never happen in this heat, if there hadn't been a break-in."

Lucy nodded. "We'll take a look and check for prints. Tell me about the workers."

"Not much to tell, Sheriff. The first was elderly, overweight, and sluggish-looking. Second one was plump also, with a red face and a wheezy voice—said he had asthma. The third was young and skinny. None of them seemed to know each other. They all worked for an outfit over in Lee County."

Lucy jotted down the name of the service and said she'd get the three workers' names. Both Valentines gave that some thought. Fran asked, "What exactly did the impostor do, while suited up?"

"Just some entertainment for the kids. Backflips, somersaults, handstands and such. Party stuff."

Lucy shook her head. "I can't figure this. Why would one of the hired workers bother to bop the guy on the head, steal his costume, and impersonate him at a difficult job? Why not just commit the robbery?"

"He probably wanted the bunny disguise in case he was spotted in the den, or entering or leaving through the window." Wentworth wearily rubbed his eyes. "As a yardworker he wouldn't have known none of the guests would be inside, and for that matter, one of the family could've seen him also."

"He's right," Fran said. Another silence passed, as everyone considered that.

"The only thing was," Wentworth said, "I remember that the rabbit suit—it was thick and heavy—looked too tight across his chest. As if it was the real performer."

The sheriff perked up. "That sounds like our thief must've been one of the first two suspects. The larger guys."

Wentworth nodded his agreement.

"Not necessarily," Fran said. "I can't see an old chubby dude doing acrobatics in this kind of heat."

"That's true," Lucy said.

"I also can't picture the second worker, someone who wheezed every breath, putting on a heavy costume in stifling-hot weather."

That was true too. They all exchanged looks. Frowning, Lucy said, "Are you saying—"

"I think the thief—and bunny rabbit—was the third workman."

"But that's impossible," Wentworth said. "How could he, on the spur of the moment, make a skinny body fill out a big man's costume?"

"There's one way," Fran said.

"What's that?"

Solution in next month's issue ...

SOLUTION TO MARCH'S YOU-SOLVE-IT

So Noted by Laird Long

"What!?" Goodwaithe exploded.

"What leads you to believe that, Sheriff?" Deputy Clemens added.

Purdy held up the Christmas card. "The simple method of contraction. The 'suicide note' uses the contractions 'can't' and 'isn't,' while Jonathon Stander's Christmas card to his brother does not—'cannot' and 'is not' are used. That tells me someone other than Stander wrote the note, in an attempt to make a murder look like a suicide. Mr. Goodwaithe here is the only one who could've done it."

The Sheriff gazed at the apoplectic man. "*Isn't* that right, or *is it not*?"

MYSTERY MAGAZINE

SUBSCRIBE TO THE WORLD'S MOST-READ MONTHLY MYSTERY MAGAZINE FOR A FEW DOLLARS PER MONTH!

THE FUTURE OF SHORT MYSTERY FICTION

Subscribe to digital issues at MysteryMagazine.ca or buy paperback issues on Amazon.

Read mysteries on your phone by visiting mysterymagazine.ca/app

ANNUAL DIGITAL SUBSCRIPTION
$29.95 USD

LIMITED TIME OFFER

Manufactured by Amazon.ca
Bolton, ON